"You're not a prince."

"One better," Mateo said, studying her eyes. "I'm your king."

The way he said it was possessive and primal enough to send a zing of electricity through Jessica. Struggling with the urge to lean into him, she didn't know what she thought she was doing, moving around a ballroom floor as if she was dancing. "There's no music."

He laughed. "Okay." He began to sing the music of "The Blue Danube" with "Da da da da da...da da, da da."

Their slight moves became the wide, swirling motions of a waltz.

And it felt wonderful. Before she could stop herself, she wished for a full skirt to bell out when they twirled. She wished for real music and the noise of a crowd celebrating in this beautiful room.

He reached the end of the song, and when his humming came to an end, he stopped dancing. She caught his gaze. Expecting to see laughter there, she smiled. But he didn't. His dark eyes searched hers. A shower of tingles rained through her. Her chest tightened.

T0357706

Dear Reader,

What a treat you're in for!

Secret Fling with the King was such a fun book to write, but it was also an honest one. Emotions run high when there are secrets to be kept and people to protect. So it's a surprise to both King Mateo and his personal assistant, Jessica, when a romance that was supposed to be just for fun blossoms into real love.

Jessica Smith, who's been in hiding to protect her daughter, couldn't be the right match for a king. Could she? He's always in the limelight and she needs to avoid attention. Especially when someone in the palace doesn't want Jessica staying around any longer than she has to as temporary replacement for the king's personal assistant.

You'll laugh reading this one. You also might gasp a time or two. But in the end, you'll be smitten with this second-chance-at-love story where love has to work really hard to conquer all.

Susan

SECRET FLING WITH THE KING

SUSAN MEIER

ROMANCE

ROMANCE

ISBN-13: 978-1-335-21633-5

Secret Fling with the King

Recycling programs for this product may not exist in your area.

Harlequin Enterprises ULC
22 Adelaide St. West, 41st Floor
Toronto, Ontario M5H 4E3, Canada
www.Harlequin.com

Printed in U.S.A.

A onetime legal secretary and director of a charitable foundation, **Susan Meier** found her bliss when she became a full-time novelist for Harlequin. She's visited ski lodges and candy factories for "research" and works in her pajamas. But the real joy of her job is creating stories about women for women. With over eighty published novels, she's tackled issues like infertility, losing a child and becoming widowed, and worked through them with her characters.

Books by Susan Meier

Harlequin Romance

A Billion-Dollar Family

Tuscan Summer with the Billionaire
The Billionaire's Island Reunion
The Single Dad's Italian Invitation

Scandal at the Palace

His Majesty's Forbidden Fling
Off-Limits to the Rebel Prince
Claiming His Convenient Princess

The Bridal Party

It Started with a Proposal
Mother of the Bride's Second Chance
One-Night Baby with the Best Man

Reunited Under the Mistletoe
One-Night Baby to Christmas Proposal
Fling with the Reclusive Billionaire

Visit the Author Profile page
at Harlequin.com for more titles.

For my crazy grandsons, who are bundles of love

CHAPTER ONE

"WE HAVE A SITUATION, SIRE."

King Mateo Stepanov adjusted the knot of his gold tie in the full-length mirror, frowning at Leon Novak's reflection directly behind his. The short bespectacled man could have been a lawyer or an accountant. Instead, he headed the human resources department for the Eastern European kingdom of Pocetak. He was good enough at his job that everyone ignored his whining.

"And what's that, Leon?"

"You know Arthur Dragan is on leave."

He checked his thick black hair in the mirror before he gave his vest a quick tug to make sure it was in place. "Emergency gallbladder surgery. Yes. I know. I got the report. And I'm assuming that's why you're here. Someone needs to replace him for the few weeks he's out."

"He's actually requested two months' leave of absence."

Mateo turned to face Leon directly. Because he towered over him, he modulated his voice to keep from sounding threatening. "Two months? I thought that surgery was easy now. One or two weeks of recovery time."

Leon winced. "He wants to relax a bit with his family."

"I see." He thought for a second. "And the reason you're here instead of his replacement is that you're preparing me for that replacement." He frowned. "It's someone I'm not going to like."

"Honestly, I think you'll like her."

"Her? My *personal* assistant is a woman?"

"You have two problems here, sire. First, she's next in line seniority wise, and your position on gender equality is strong. You can't prevent a woman from taking a job she's entitled to."

"Artie and I go over my schedule while I'm dressing. Just like you and I are talking now. In my dressing room."

"That's because he was your nanny before he was your personal assistant. That was a very convenient shift of jobs for him and you."

"When I was thirteen, I no longer needed a nanny and did need an assistant."

"And it worked out beautifully," Leon agreed.

"Yes. It did."

Leon waited a second, then carefully said, "Are you saying you can't work with a woman?"

"Of course, I can work with a woman! There are women in my security team, and I have a cabinet and a hierarchy of royals who aren't all men!"

He took a breath, then grabbed his jacket from the valet stand and slid into it. Though it was mid-April and the trees had begun to get leaves, temperatures could still be cool enough to warrant a jacket. "It'll cut an hour off our time together, but I'll be fully dressed before she enters my quarters. But that's all the compromise I'm making. She'll meet me in the dining room when I'm eating breakfast, and we'll go over my schedule then."

Leon breathed an obvious sigh of relief. "Very good, sire."

"And I'm not so difficult that you had to fear telling me. I might like things a certain way, but I'm not obstinate."

"No, you're not. But nonetheless let me suggest you relax before I tell you issue number two."

"Issue number two?"

"I told you there were two problems with Arthur's replacement. The second one is that she is Eleanore Smith's mother."

"Who's Eleanore Smith—Wait! Isn't she the woman who testified against that American politician who was found guilty of drugging and sexually assaulting her? What was it? Ten years ago?"

"Yes."

He fell to the Queen Anne chair beside the small desk in his dressing room. "Ouch."

"If you give her mother the position—for a mere two months while Arthur is on sabbatical this spring—you won't go against your very public fight for gender equality. But if the press discovers she's Jessica Smith, Eleanore Smith's mother, there might be…*conversations*. Articles. Podcasts. Still, if you don't give her the job and the press discovers that you blocked her from a promotion she deserves, that opens the original can of worms."

"So, we're damned if we don't but only potentially damned if we do."

"Yes."

Mateo shook his head. "That situation was ten years ago."

"Doesn't matter to the press."

"And the subject of all the publicity wasn't Jessica herself. It was her daughter. Plus, nothing about that case affects me. Not personally. Not politically."

"The press won't care. There will be publicity. Questions. It will disrupt our days and the palace privacy. There will be reporters at the gates. Rabid reporters hoping to make it into a story."

He thought that through. He remembered the days after his wife died. How reporters scrambled to get pictures of him or his kids. There was nothing worse than scrutiny from the press when you were suffering.

Still, no one knew how to keep a secret better than royalty.

"If you take this to its logical conclusion, the problem revolves around the press finding out that she's Eleanore Smith's mother. Meaning the chance exists that they won't find out."

Leon winced. "Typically, we put out a press release when there's a staff change."

"Seriously? For every darned position?"

"Yes. People like their jobs here so much that it's usually a list of lower-level or entry-level positions, or employees who are being promoted to the next rung on the ladder. And because it's usually maids, gardeners, motor pool workers, I doubt anyone reads it. She was on that list when she was hired. No one investigated."

"But this position interacts with me. Someone will look into her. All it takes is one zealous reporter, desperate to make a mark, for our secret to be out." He thought for a second. "Give her the job, but don't announce it."

"The press is accustomed to—"

"Did Arthur do a press release about having gallbladder surgery?"

"It was an emergency surgery. I doubt he had time. But we should—"

"We *should* nothing. The woman deserves the job. That's the end of the matter as far as I'm concerned. You, on the other hand, would like to put out a press release. As your king I'm telling you not to. See? Problem solved."

Jessica Smith sat in the waiting room for the king's suite of offices, not sure if she should be excited or fearful. An opportunity to work directly with the king was almost unheard-of. The steno pool might type, line edit or proofread his documents, but they never interacted with him. Their work was delivered by Pete Franklin, the security guard who acted as receptionist/gatekeeper for the king's private office or Arthur Dragan, the king's assistant.

When King Mateo turned thirteen, Arthur—his nanny—became his personal assistant, and the man never left the job. Technically, seventy-four wasn't too old to be working. But the unintended consequence of employing the same staff for at least two decades was that the king would be expecting things to be done a certain way. He was probably so accustomed to his routine that she'd be jumping to keep up with him.

She wanted the job anyway.

With a deep breath for courage, she looked around at the sedate reception area. White woodwork. Shiny floor tiles. Medallion light fixture. An antique mahogany desk where pretty redhaired Molly, the receptionist for this part of the building, sat focused on a report she was reading.

The silence of the place made her nerves jangle. There were enough receptionists and guards that no one stood a chance of getting to the king unnoticed—not that she was trying to sneak in. She'd been invited. But she'd never been beyond her own section of the palace offices. *No one* entered the executive suite except the king's direct staff and esteemed visitors. Only cabinet and in-person meetings were held in his private conference room. The king himself didn't roam the halls. He didn't pace, thinking through sticky diplomatic situations. He stayed secluded.

An office employee for over five years, she'd never met the big boss. She simply did the technical work on his decrees, memos, letters and sometimes treaties and agreements.

The door opened. Molly glanced over.

Leon said, "The king will see Ms. Smith now."

Her heart tumbled. She'd been a legal assistant most of her adult life. A fluke had gotten her a job in the palace and three or four unexpected moves had put her in a position to replace Arthur.

She was about to meet *a king*.

She rose from her seat, straightened her simple sheath dress and walked toward Leon.

He stepped away from the door, motioning for her to go down the forbidden hall. "Right this way."

She left the segment of the building that was the original palace built in the seventeen hundreds and entered the long corridor leading to the new wing. Gone were the woodwork and shiny tiles, replaced by elegant hardwood floors and walls of arched windows that displayed leafy green trees and colorful flower gardens outside.

Three steps took them up to the next level. They

turned right, then left, then right again. Leon opened a door and stepped aside for her to enter first.

Tall, muscular Pete Franklin rose. "Good morning, Leon." He nodded at Jessica. "Jessica." He motioned to the door behind him. "The king is expecting you."

Leon said, "Thank you," as he opened the door.

She took a silent breath to steady her nerves and followed him into the huge office. She anticipated bookshelves and dark paneling with heavy velvet drapes. Instead, the room had a pale sofa and chair, a simple modern desk with two chairs for visitors, and two walls of glass, again displaying the grounds outside. White drapes had been opened and stood bunched in the corners. He probably needed them for the afternoon sun. But mornings were perfect for sitting in the big, almost empty room, and communing with nature.

The chair behind the desk swiveled to face them. The king, tall, gorgeous, dark-haired Mateo Stepanov, rose.

She knew better than to curtsey—palace employees had a special dispensation to keep the level of bowing and curtseying from interrupting work—though she desperately wanted to. In a black suit with a gold tie and vest, King Mateo went beyond imposing to magnificent.

"King Mateo, this is Jessica Smith." Leon faced Jessica. "Jessica Smith, this is your king, Mateo Stepanov."

He bowed slightly. "Ms. Smith."

The urge to curtesy was so strong that she had to fight it. But because he'd bowed slightly, she let herself mimic the move. "Your Majesty."

"Please have a seat."

She sat on one of the two chairs in front of his desk. Leon sat on the other and the king lowered himself to his seat behind the desk.

"You are the one in line to replace Arthur while he is on leave. But we have an issue."

Her muscles tightened. Her breath froze. Anger rippled through her. Not anger with the king, anger with her daughter's situation. Like a certain White House intern who lost all chance for a normal life after an incident with the US president, Eleanore's life had changed completely. She'd been drugged, raped and held at an estate until she was "debriefed" and allowed to leave, but questions still swirled around the incident. Even after the perpetrator was convicted and sentenced to twenty years in prison, Eleanore's account of the events was doubted. She had been twenty, old enough to consent, and the beloved politician swore she'd consented. After he was convicted, she'd had to change her name and leave her country to find any peace.

Yet even after all these years, somehow that incident managed to find its way into Jessica's life. She'd stopped using her first name and began using her middle name, but apparently the scandal had found her.

Again.

"Arthur and I had certain routines and rituals that we'll have to change for you."

Shocked when King Mateo began talking about the job, not her daughter's troubles, she said, "I don't see why. I'm as capable as Arthur."

"Arthur and I ran over the day's schedule while I was dressing in the morning." He winced. "If a day was particularly busy, we'd do it while I was showering. I'm sure you'd prefer me fully clothed."

"Fully clothed would be better." Her cheeks pinkened. A shadowy vision of her going over the king's schedule while he was naked under the spray of his shower popped into her head. He was tall and fit. Everyone knew he worked out three days a week and jogged in the evenings after most of the staff was gone.

The shadowy vision sharpened and became more real. She envisioned his well-defined muscles with rivulets of water sliding along smooth skin. Her mouth went dry.

She shook herself back to reality. Blaming her weird thoughts on the pressure of meeting a king, she pulled herself together. She was a fifty-two-year-old woman who had gone through every second of her daughter's trauma with her. She'd divorced Eleanore's father when he'd hedged questions with the press, making things worse. She worked to support herself, always paid her own way. She never got flummoxed. She wouldn't start today just because the guy she was talking to was a handsome king, who went over his schedule while dressing. He'd already said some things would change. This was probably one of them. That was undoubtedly why he'd brought it up.

She straightened in her chair.

He laughed. "Relax, please, Ms. Smith. I wanted to give you an idea of how we'll both be adjusting to our situation, not just you."

She nodded. "Okay."

"You and I will meet while I'm eating breakfast. Meaning, you will come into my dining room. Though there are times I will require assistance with the choice of clothing for specific meetings or events, those moments we will be in my dressing room. Additionally, there are documents we can consult about what should be worn where. Arthur kept copious notes."

She nodded, finally understanding that a personal assistant's job was quite different than an office assistant. There was no dividing line between his life and his work. He lived at his job. He *was* his job. What he wore, what he ate, where he went—everything meant something.

That's what she would be dealing with. That was the shift in her thinking that had to be made. She might not have to read his schedule to him while he showered but it was her job to keep him on track. Both professionally and personally. No more typing, editing or proofreading documents.

Leon rose. "If there's nothing else, sire…"

The king rose and Jessica scrambled to her feet.

"That's all, Leon." He faced Jessica. "You and I have a schedule to go over."

Her chest froze. She displayed her empty hands. "I don't have anything."

Leon said, "The king's schedule has been emailed to you, along with his calendar and all appropriate phone numbers. You will also receive an access code to a spreadsheet with confidential phone numbers and emails."

With that, Leon turned and left. Her gaze followed him until the door closed on him, then she faced the king.

The king.

He smiled. "Leon never says a spare word."

She took a breath. "No. He doesn't."

"And he can be a bit stuffy."

She fought a laugh. "Yes."

"I'm not stuffy." He motioned for her to sit again. "Out of necessity, the office atmosphere is sedate." He glanced around. "Honestly, sometimes the place is weirdly quiet."

She looked around the way he had. "I see that."

"But there will also be times when my family arrives unannounced." He winced. "When they were kids, they'd sometimes barge in fighting."

She laughed.

"As a personal assistant, you might be required to help with that. Sometimes to divert their attention." He pointed outside. "Oh, look, it's warm out. Why don't you go swimming?"

She snickered.

"You laugh, but that one worked with my kids until they became teenagers. Now, it's more things like fighting over who gets the Bentley."

"Yes, Your Majesty."

"You'll get a feel for when you should intervene and when you should step back and let them rant. There'll also be times when they want to come in and lounge around. If my schedule allows it," his voice softened, "I like having them here."

She smiled at the affection in his tone. His wife had died several years ago when his oldest daughter was about eighteen. Technically, he'd raised his kids through the hardest part of their lives alone.

"I imagine it's difficult being a single dad when you're a king."

"I think anyone who works from home has the same problems."

She considered that. "It sounds the same but it's not."

He relaxed in his chair. "That's probably true. But I want you to get comfortable with the fact that you're allowed to shoo them out, as long as you do it tactfully. Also, if you observe something, like if one of the kids seems moody and I'm not catching it, you're allowed to speak up." He smiled. "You simply might have to wait until the child in question isn't in the room."

"Got it. I know all about raising kids. I have a daughter."

The word *daughter* fell into the room like a brick. If he noticed, he didn't mention it or bring up Eleanore's situation. Probably because he had troubles of his own and work to do and her daughter was irrelevant.

Her brain froze. Had she found a place where her daughter's troubles really were old news?

Lord, she hoped so.

He smiled again and her breath stalled. With his dark hair and dark eyes, and a face that was just a bit rugged, he was about the sexiest man she'd ever met. And he wasn't a bully or a tyrant. He seemed like a nice guy.

It was going to be a struggle not to stutter in his presence, let alone to keep herself one step ahead of him so that he was always prepared.

But she'd never had a chance like this and probably wouldn't get one again.

She had to make it work.

CHAPTER TWO

MATEO CAUGHT HIMSELF staring at the woman sitting in front of his desk and shook his head to clear it. Gorgeous women weren't uncommon in the world of royalty, but this woman wasn't painted and primped. Her dark hair fell to her shoulders and was nicely shaped around her face. Her clear blue eyes seemed to see everything at once, a good quality for someone who had to adjust to this busy environment and help him get through his days. But there was also a softness in those pale blue orbs that intrigued him. The simple dress she wore might have been designed to play down her figure, but sometimes there was no hiding gentle curves.

He handed her an electronic tablet. "This is mine. You can use it to go over the schedule."

She looked at it as if she thought it would bite her. "Yours? Are you sure I should be touching that. Aren't there state secrets in there or something?"

He laughed. "No. The only things in this particular tablet are addresses, phone numbers and schedules. You'll actually be using Arthur's tablet, which is at his desk, but for now, we'll go over the schedule with mine."

She nodded and slowly lowered her gaze to the tablet. "Okay."

"So, this morning I have two phone calls, followed by an in-office meeting."

She tapped the tablet a few times.

The schedule appeared on the screen, as it was programmed to do. He swore he saw her sigh with relief.

"The phone numbers for both of this morning's calls are beside the names."

She slowly looked up from the screen. "Got it. Thank you."

Their gazes caught and he watched her cheeks turn red. She couldn't be embarrassed. Nothing embarrassing had happened—

But she might be attracted to him.

He almost snorted. That was wishful thinking. Only a certain kind of woman was attracted to a man in power, a man whose whole life was fodder for the press. After experiencing the pressure of the media in her daughter's situation, she probably was not that kind of woman.

Which was too bad. She was so pretty and seemed so normal. Especially for a person who'd gone through a crisis with her daughter the way she had.

All of which was none of his business. Though she was allowed to step into his life and maneuver things around, including his children, her private life was off-limits to him.

He pointed to the right. "Arthur's office is through that door. You place the calls the way you would for any boss. Then buzz me and I'll pick up."

"Yes. Good. I did this all the time when I worked for lawyers."

"That's why you're here."

She rose from the chair and walked into Arthur's office. Then stopped, turned and walked the tablet back to him. "Sorry. You know, for future reference you might want to let Leon explain these kinds of things to new employees."

"What would the fun be in that?"

She blinked, then laughed.

"I used these little tasks to help you get accustomed to me. I know it's weird to work with a king."

She smiled. Her entire face softened. Her pretty blue eyes met his. "I guess that's smart."

He leaned toward her and whispered, "Trust me. It is. I am a king. I know things."

She chuckled, turned and left his office.

He sat back in his chair abundantly pleased with himself. Showing new employees the ropes wasn't his normal way of getting them comfortable working with him. But because Jessica would be working with him for so long, he'd wanted to meet her and talk to her before promises were made. Just in case her situation with her daughter had soured her. Now, he was glad he had. She was nice. Pretty. She also didn't scare easily.

He was extremely pleased with Jessica Smith—

Maybe too pleased. It might be because of her age, but he felt unexpectedly comfortable with her. The kind of comfortable a man feels with a friend—

Or a woman he was interested in.

He held back a wince. That was actually the problem. There was something about her that made him want to flirt. And that was wrong. A smart boss—even a king—knew that getting romantically involved with an employee was nothing but trouble.

But, boy, she was tempting.

When his phone rang, he assumed it was Jessica with one of his two calls on the line. "Yes?"

"I'm sorry, Your Majesty," Jessica said. "But Molly just called me. Your son is on the way back to your office."

"I told you they come by unannounced."

"Should I open the door and eavesdrop?"

He laughed. "No. Joshua is still in law school, but he also works in the government. He might simply have a question. Get those calls for me. If he's here to chat, I can use that to ease him out.

Besides, my schedule's tight with the ambassador coming. Can't let him dillydally."

"Yes, Your Majesty."

He hung up the phone just as the main door to his office swung open and his son strode in.

"We have a problem." Tall and dark-haired, Joshua began to pace. "Sabrina's been drinking and clubbing again."

Mateo knew his eighteen-year-old daughter was going through a fun phase, just as Olivia—his oldest daughter and heir to the throne—and Joshua had when they entered university.

"I know your sister's underage, Joshua, but let's not panic."

Joshua spun to face his desk. "Panic? There's a picture of her flashing her breasts in a club." He combed his fingers through his hair. "She is turned away from the camera. But it's clear what she's doing. Especially since her shirt is halfway up her back."

Mateo barely controlled his anger. "Damn it." He now understood why Joshua was so upset. She'd crossed "the" line.

"In her defense," Josh said, "cameras aren't allowed in that club. She had a reasonable expectation of privacy."

Mateo tossed his pen to his desk. "We *never* have an expectation of privacy." He sighed. "You've seen the picture?"

"No. A friend called to tell me about it. It only

went out to a select group of friends—people Mike Conrad knows," he said, referring to one of the friends in his social group. "And because it doesn't show anything, it probably won't go any further. But I think it illustrates a pattern of behavior."

Mateo took a second to wonder about his decision to send his son to law school because everything turned into a legal matter to him, then said, "Get her down here." He sucked in a breath. Remembering he had an ambassador arriving within the hour, he changed his mind. "No. I'll go up to her."

He rose from his seat and walked to Jessica Smith's door. Opening it a crack, he said, "Don't place those calls. I have to go upstairs to the family quarters. I'll let you know when I return."

She nodded.

He strode to Sabrina's room. He didn't even knock, just opened the door and walked in. "What in the name of all that is holy do you think you were doing flashing at a club!"

She winced. Average height with black hair like his and her mother's green eyes, she blinked innocently. "I had no idea someone had a camera."

"We've had this conversation before. It doesn't matter if there's a camera or not. You *never* do anything like that. If the press gets ahold of that shot, it will take you *years* to fix your reputation, if we can even fix it at all! You better pray that picture stays private."

The innocent blink became puppy-dog eyes. "Or you could make sure that it does. I know the security department has sources who could find out who took it, and you could get it back."

"It's digital! It's almost impossible to simply take it back like a print photo. Besides, I shouldn't have to get it back."

"You're right. Cameras aren't allowed in that club." She pursed her lips. "Maybe we can have the person who took it banned from the club, so we'll know it will never happen again."

Though his anger subsided a bit, frustration began to replace it. "You are missing the point."

"Or maybe *you're* missing the point. You never take my side. Never defend me. Everything is always my fault!"

"Your behavior is supposed to be above reproach."

She sighed and shook her head. "That's right. It's always me."

His frustration grew. He couldn't tell if she was being deliberately obtuse or if she genuinely didn't understand that her life was different. Her brother and sister didn't fully appreciate it until they hit their twenties. But they also weren't as uninhibited as she seemed to be.

The phone in his jacket pocket rang. He reached for it. "What!"

"I'm sorry, Your Majesty," Jessica Smith said. "But the French ambassador is here early."

He took a breath, working to get himself into a better frame of mind. He could not greet an ambassador while he was angry. "I'll be right down."

"Would you like me to get him set up in the conference room?"

He took another breath. "Yes. He loves coffee. The kitchen would have prepared his favorite. By the time he's in the conference room, his coffee will be there. That'll amuse him for a while."

"Thank you, sir."

"I'll be right down."

He disconnected the call and looked at his daughter. If she really was confused, somewhere along the way he'd missed teaching her something. He had to fix that. "This isn't resolved. We'll talk again tonight."

"I have plans for tonight."

He headed for the door. "Cancel them."

When the king walked through Jessica's office to go into the conference room where the French ambassador awaited him, his behavior had gone from congenial to almost silent with overtones of anger. He tried to hide that when he greeted the ambassador, but she saw it.

After closing the door on the conference room, she returned to her desk and took out the policies and procedures manual that Arthur must have created thirty years ago because the pages were tattered and dry. She'd looked for an updated copy in his computer and tablet but there wasn't one. Probably because the guy knew his job so well, he didn't need it.

Still, she did. She'd worked in offices most of her life, but she'd never been a *personal* assistant. The easy way King Mateo had mentioned her helping choose clothes for events and shooing his kids out of his office showed her she didn't fully understand the scope of this job. Old or not, this was the only guide she had. Specifics might have changed but the big things probably remained the same.

Flipping through the pages, she found the dress code section with details of which of his uniforms were to be worn when. But there were also line items about making sure he had a clean and pressed tux for formal affairs and affording him a choice of shirt. Housecleaning would provide soaps, shampoos, clean towels, and do his laundry, but it was up to her to make sure the clothes he needed were ready to wear when he needed them.

She looked up from the book. She supposed that made sense.

There were pages of birthdays of dignitaries and holidays of other countries so she could help the king send greetings to the appropriate people on the correct day. In the back were lists of his favorite dishes, things he liked to eat for lunch and even recipes in case the cook left and sabotaged the recipe bank by stealing the instructions for making the king's favorite foods.

That made her snicker. Arthur was one suspicious old man.

But she got the picture. While the king was in meetings like this, she could sneak away with the tablet containing his schedule and take a look at his closet, his clothes, to assure the suit or uniform he needed was ready when he needed it. The man had visitors every day. It shouldn't be too difficult to find a few minutes to check his wardrobe.

The group broke for lunch, which Mateo and the French ambassador ate in the king's dining room. She took advantage of that time to slide into his enormous closet.

Dark and formal with cherrywood shelving between rows of suits and uniforms, shirts, sweaters and trousers, the place reminded her of a dungeon. Ignoring that, she looked at uniforms and formal wear that dated back a century and decided that at some point she would catalog them. He also had at least a hundred pairs of shoes.

Aside from a ball over the weekend—for which there were several clean tuxes—he didn't really have any outside-the-office events, so she scurried downstairs and was at her desk when they returned from their break.

They spent another four hours behind the closed doors of the conference room. After the French ambassador left, King Mateo asked her to come into his office to get instructions for some work she would be doing the next day. All the laughter was gone from his voice. It was as if their pleasant beginnings that morning hadn't happened.

When he was done explaining the two projects, he said, "That's all for the day. I'll see you tomorrow."

She headed to her office, but a weird sense hit her two seconds before she would have walked over the threshold. He'd gotten angry after his son had come into his office and raced up to the family suite. He'd said his son wouldn't be a problem, but what if he had been?

She stopped and turned around, retracing her steps to his desk. "Is everything okay?"

He glanced up. His deep brown eyes caught her gaze. Attraction zinged through her. In pictures he was impressive. In person, he was breathtaking. Serious, yet sexy. Ruggedly handsome. Everybody he came into contact with was probably attracted to him. Accepting that made it easier to ignore the little fizzles that raced along her skin.

"Everything's fine."

His eyes said the opposite.

He'd said she could interfere if one of his kids needed to be eased out of his office or if she noticed one of the kids was moody. Right now, he was the one who was moody. From the open way he'd spoken that morning, it was clear he would be honest if he wanted or needed her help. Since he'd told her everything was fine, she would take that as his way of telling her not to probe any further.

She smiled, said, "Good night," and left, the way a good assistant is supposed to.

The next morning, she arrived at the palace, ready to go to work. During his after-lunch session with the ambassador the day before, she had played with Arthur's tablet and laptop, and knew how to get to everything from the king's schedule to lists of phone numbers and names of foreign dignitaries. She hadn't forgotten the two calls she was supposed to place the day before but couldn't because the ambassador arrived early. That would be the first thing she'd remind him.

Coat in her office closet, tablet in hand, she made her way to the king's quarters. A maid greeted her and led her to the dining room, which was as formal and stuffy as his dressing room had been. A long cherrywood table sat in the middle of the room in front of a matching buffet. A silver tea service which she suspected held coffee sat on the corner nearest to the king. Pale blue floral wallpaper covered the space above the wainscoting. A huge chandelier dripped elegant crystals.

He rose as she entered. "Good morning, Ms. Smith." He motioned to the chair kitty-corner to his. "Have a seat."

Much to her relief, his voice let her know that the mood from the evening before had improved.

"Good morning, Your Majesty."

"Have you eaten?"

"Yes."

"Well, tomorrow, save your appetite. I've asked the cook to make blueberry pancakes. You won't want to miss that."

She laughed and he smiled at her. The wonderful ripples of attraction she always felt around him spiraled through her. Because they were wrong and pointless, she forced her thoughts onto the work they needed to do.

Though she was becoming troubled by them. Usually, when she told herself something was wrong or off-limits, her feelings fell in line. But she could not seem to stop her attraction or even minimize it.

Still, this was only her second day. Surely, it would soon begin to shrink until it disappeared into nothing.

They put the two calls he'd missed the day before on the top of his to-do list for the day. Then they went through his schedule. That sorted, he reminded her of the work he'd given her to do before she'd gone home the day before.

When she would have risen and left him to finish his breakfast, his eighteen-year-old daughter burst into the dining room. Wearing jeans, a T-shirt and flip-flops, she glared at her father. "You've suspended my motor pool privileges?"

He set his napkin on his plate. "I told you to stay in last night so we could have a discussion. You went against a direct order."

"A direct order! I'm not one of your subjects."

He sighed. "Actually, you are. You are also my daughter. Your privileges are suspended until we have that talk."

She rolled her eyes and sighed heavily. "Whatever!" Then she stormed out of the room.

Mateo shook his head. "That was my youngest."

She knew that from pictures in the press. But their conversation the day before about his family suddenly took meaning and she understood why he had warned her. If his daughter had done this in the king's office, she'd have first closed the doors so no one could hear her. Then she would have started timing. After five minutes, she would have interrupted with a phone call.

"Sabrina, right? I've seen pictures."

"She is turning out to be more of a handful than my other two kids put together."

Jessica pressed her lips together to keep from laughing. He didn't look forlorn or angry. He appeared to be out of his element. "I've heard that happens with the baby of the family."

"Her mother would have been infuriated. Instead of losing motor pool privileges, Princess Sabrina probably would have been grounded for a month."

"Why don't you do that?"

"Ground her for a month?" He winced. "She would be like a bear with a thorn in its paw! That would be punishment for me, not her."

"Okay. Make it two weeks…or a week." She shrugged. "Punishment has to hurt, but also if she's hanging around the palace that gives you time to talk to her." She smiled. "I can fix your schedule so that you could have lunch with her or TV time at night…or riding time. I know you both go out riding. Maybe do that together?"

He smiled. "I see what you're doing."

"What? Giving you time to chitchat with her and not lecture?"

He chuckled. "That's pretty smart."

Lifting her tablet, she rose from the table. "I'll look at your schedule and talk to the people in the stables."

"Thank you."

She nodded. "You're welcome."

Her job suddenly fell into place. Giving him a little advice now and again wouldn't be difficult. She didn't have to probe or overstep. She simply had to make a suggestion or two. She could choose his clothes, keep his wardrobe clean and ready to wear, remind him of appointments, birthdays and anything he needed to know.

Piece of cake.

Unfortunately, considering her attraction, she worried that assuming so many personal roles in his life might cause it to grow. But she dismissed that thought. She was a *personal* assistant. Not just help in the office. Plus, she knew her attraction stemmed from the fact that the king was attractive and normal—

Well, darn. That *was* why it wasn't going away. He was normal. Likeable. If he were stuffy, the way he sometimes appeared in public, or arrogant, the way a lot of royals could be, or pretentious, she could have easily dismissed him.

But he was likable.

Good-looking and likable.

And if she didn't get control of this she would be in big trouble.

CHAPTER THREE

SHE LEFT THE dining room and Mateo forced his attention to his breakfast.

Arthur probably would have told him to lock Sabrina in her quarters for a month and only let her out for dinner. Jessica had given him a usable suggestion. His appreciation for her as an assistant grew, even as something personal inside him shimmied with understanding. He liked her. He liked that she wasn't afraid of him or hesitant. He liked that she gave him suggestions without being overbearing.

He also liked that she was extremely pretty and appeared to be very soft.

That observation forced him back to reality. He didn't get involved at all with staff. Except his assistant. In that case, they had to be somewhat personal. She saw everything in his life. Even in a short two months she would get to know his children, his likes and dislikes and pick out his clothes and help him plan menus.

If he didn't figure out a way to stop noticing

how pretty she was and how they sort of fit as people, it wouldn't affect his life as much as it would hers. After his disastrous first marriage to a pampered princess who liked being a queen more than she liked him, he had vowed never to marry again. Anything he might have with Jessica wouldn't go beyond a romance. And she seemed to be the kind of person who wanted more—who might need more—meaning anything between them would hurt her because it would end.

Not to mention what getting romantically involved would do to their work. He needed her as an assistant, and she probably needed this job.

He would keep his distance.

After his Wednesday morning ride with Sabrina provided him with the perfect opportunity to talk to her in a pleasant atmosphere, he saw even more the value of Jessica Smith. With the state Sabrina was in, and his responsibility to lead his daughter into her next phase of life, he couldn't afford to lose an assistant who seemed to have really good ideas about addressing his daughter's behavior.

He returned to his office all business. Thursday, he could have been the Pope, he was so respectful and professional. Friday morning, they did most of their communicating at breakfast before he had a long list of meetings.

Friday evening, she poked her head into his office, he thought, to say good-night. Before she spoke, he looked up and smiled. "Thank you. We had a good first week. Enjoy your weekend."

"I will. But I'm told you need to go down to the ballroom and sign off on everything for the ball tomorrow night for your son's twenty-second birthday."

Signing off on the ballroom setup was something his deceased wife had put into play when the staff inadvertently used the wrong silverware. He hadn't believed anyone had noticed. She'd had a hissy fit.

He rose. "We're going to have to change that rule."

"I'll put it on your calendar."

"Thank you. And by the way, you come with me on this final inspection."

"I do?" Her face contorted with confusion. "Why?"

"I don't know. Arthur always did. I think he used his eagle eyes to look for things I'd miss." He motioned to the door. "Which means, your job is to look around too. See if there's a goblet that doesn't match the china."

She snickered, then she frowned. "Oh, you're serious."

"My mother always said, two heads are better than one." He directed her to the door again. "Shall we?"

She shrugged. "If it's part of the job, I'm ready."

They walked down the hall to the huge ballroom. "This is another thing we added on when we renovated the palace," he said, opening a side door into the room, ushering her into the enormous space with high ceilings and rows of chandeliers, sufficient round tables to seat five hundred guests and an empty space for dancing in front of a section for a band.

She looked around in awe. "It always amazes me when you open a door."

He felt the pleasure of how she didn't monitor her reactions. She made him feel like a person, not a role. "Really? Do you think I should have minions who go before me and do that kind of stuff?"

"Yes."

He snorted. "Seriously?"

She shrugged. "What do you expect we'd think? You never interact with staff. You never even walk through that section of the building. You're so aloof sometimes our imaginations run wild."

He guffawed. "I can only imagine the rumors."

She looked around again. "This is amazing."

"And you've *never* seen it?"

They eased through the rows of round tables, glancing at silver and china. "No, Your Majesty." She peered over at him. "Do we have to measure the distance between the silverware and the plates?"

"The staff do that. They also measure the distance of each tablecloth to the floor." He grinned. "My mother taught me that."

"I think she knew the day would come when you'd be signing off on the setup."

"No. She simply liked me to understand that things didn't magically appear. The rule came about not because my late wife wanted to check everything out, but because she wanted staff to know she was watching. I trust the staff."

"Humph. So, all this is a formality?"

"I think my wife believed if they knew she was coming down to check their work they'd check it first."

She bobbed her head. "I guess it makes sense."

"It makes no sense and once we get it on my calendar, we will be getting rid of it."

They reached the end of the tables, and he turned to get a perspective of the entire dining area. "It looks perfect to me."

She sighed with appreciation. "Grand and elegant." She turned. "And I suppose this is the dance floor."

Watching her, he smiled. "Yes. It amazes me that you work in a palace that you've never seen."

"We're told that's *your* doing."

He laughed. "Again, that was my late wife. She liked the line between us and staff. Mostly because of privacy. That I understood."

"I do too. But that's why palace employees don't ever see certain things." She looked around again. "Like this gorgeous room."

"Maybe it's another rule we should reconsider

when I get the king-must-approve-ballroom rule off the roster."

She laughed, but twirled around, looking at the ceiling, as if fascinated by all the sparkle and glitter. "Just trying to envision what dancing here must feel like."

He ambled over to her. "Really?"

"Every little girl imagines being Cinderella, dancing with a prince in a glamorous room like this."

He took her hand and pulled her into a dance hold. "Then, let's give you the real feeling."

He saw her breath stutter and all but felt the warm wave of her attraction to him. She'd hid it well all week, but with her hand in his and his other hand on her waist, it was so plain he wondered how he'd missed it.

"You're not a prince."

"One better," he said, studying her eyes. "I'm your king."

The way he said it was possessive and primal enough to send a zing of electricity through her. Struggling with the urge to lean into him, she didn't know what she thought she was doing, moving around a ballroom floor as if she was dancing. "There's no music."

He laughed. "Okay." He began to sing the music of "The Blue Danube" waltz. "Da Da Da Da Da… Da Da, Da Da."

Their slight moves became the wide swirling motions of a waltz.

And it felt wonderful. Before she could stop herself, she wished for a full skirt to bell out when they twirled. She wished for real music and the noise of a crowd celebrating in this wonderful room.

He reached the end of the song and when his humming stopped, he stopped dancing. She caught his gaze. Expecting to see laughter there, she smiled. But he didn't. His dark eyes searched hers. A shower of tingles rained through her. Her chest tightened.

They were close enough that they could kiss. The temptation of it rose in her, stealing her breath with fear, even as she wished for it.

But then what? The man was a king. She wasn't a pauper, but she was a commoner. An employee of his palace. Someone who existed in his world only to make his life easier.

She took a step back.

He released her from the dance hold. "I'll phone the ballroom staff and give my approval."

"Yes, Your Majesty."

She said the title slowly, deliberately. Not just for her own benefit, but for his. There was a distance between them that couldn't be breached. Not merely because he was royal but because her life came with problems that would cause him more grief than he could imagine.

Of course, none of that would matter if they simply had a fling, nothing serious. Something no one would ever hear about.

But looking into the dark eyes of Pocetak's king, she knew this was not a frivolous man. Everything he did, he did with passion and sincerity.

She took another step back. "I'll see you on Monday."

She turned and began to walk away from him. For the first time since she'd gotten a job in the palace, she wished she hadn't. Some temptations weren't to be missed. Some were simply too delicious to walk away from. And she had a feeling this was one of them.

But he was a king, who, technically, was still raising a child—

She stopped abruptly as her brain kicked in. She pivoted to face him. "Are phones allowed in the ballroom for your parties?"

He took a few steps toward her. "Those things are confiscated at the door, so most people know not to bring them."

She glanced around the big room. "Make sure security checks everyone. I know you think that incident with Sabrina was just kids' stuff. But what if it wasn't? What if someone is either trying to undermine you or blackmail you? Has security considered that someone might have nudged Sabrina into flashing her friends at that club?"

* * *

Mateo blinked to bring himself fully into the moment. The longing to kiss her drifted away as reality forced him to be a king again. "Yes. Every possibility is discussed when something like this happens. My son is comparing the guest list for the ball to the people who were at the club."

"Your son sounds very much in control."

Mateo snorted and motioned for her to walk to the door and up the corridor. "He will run parliament when his sister is queen. They will be very effective." His nerve endings jangled from the shift of almost kissing her one minute to discussing his kids the next.

"And his sister? Olivia who will be queen? Is she ready?"

He worked to hide a smile of fatherly pride. "She's the epitome of a future ruler. She's smart, forward-thinking, and totally in control—"

He finally saw that she'd kept talking about his kids to completely end the almost-kiss moment. Not merely as a distraction, but a reminder of their different stations in life. Except what she didn't understand was that he was well aware of the uniqueness of what was happening between them. He'd never been instantly comfortable with someone the way he was with her. People had to work their way into his good graces to gain trust. Her past had made her into someone special, and even as it made him curious, the attraction added a layer of something that made the comfort level risky.

Not because he should be afraid of her. Because she would never want this life. Anything they had would go nowhere.

He stopped walking. "You go on ahead. I'm taking the stairs to my quarters. Have a lovely weekend."

She smiled at him. "Enjoy your son's birthday."

He took a step backward, reminding himself that limiting his time with her was for her benefit and a good king looked after his subjects. "I'm sure we will."

With that she turned and walked away.

He didn't damn his station in life. He didn't wish to be someone else. But he did wonder what it would be like to be in a relationship with someone like her. Someone authentic. Someone as soft as silk—having held her as they danced, he knew that now. Someone who made his heart skip a beat.

CHAPTER FOUR

WALKING UP THE stairs to her fourth-floor apartment, Jessica scolded herself, annoyed that she'd let things go a little too far when they danced in the ballroom. Gazing into each other's eyes? Feeling a connection, a rightness?

She winced. That might actually have been more than a little too far.

Of course, he'd started it.

She fought the urge to roll her eyes at the silly, primary-school comeback. Her brain wanted to be happy and frivolous. It didn't want logic and reality disturbing the memory, the moment. She'd felt young and free when she'd danced with the king, more like herself than she had in years. She'd lost a chunk of her life fighting alongside her daughter. Then she'd more or less gone into hiding. It felt good to just be herself again.

She carted her groceries up the last flight of stairs and dug out her apartment key. Feeling young and free or not, a king was still a king— not someone she should be dancing with. She'd successfully gotten them out of the situation when her brain had switched on and made the connection between the picture taken of his daughter and the ball occurring the following night and she'd reminded him that security had to be aware.

But for ten minutes or so, they'd fallen into something that was pure joy. A private conversation. A short dance. And a wonderful longing to kiss.

The kiss hadn't happened, but hadn't someone once said that anticipation was better than actually getting what you wanted?

Opening her door, she frowned. Anticipation might be fun but kissing Mateo would have been better.

She grimaced at her use of his first name and reminded herself of her life goals. Retiring to a quiet cottage in the country. Privacy. Gardening. Flying to Brazil to visit her grandkids once her daughter gave her some. That was her endgame. Flirting with a king could derail that if she wasn't careful.

Walking her groceries to her kitchen island, she heard the sound of someone climbing up the steps, and knew it was probably the guy who lived across the hall, Bob Greenburg. He was a transplant from the States. Nice guy. Always considerate. Never once asked her about her daughter or her job. Not a nosy bone in his body.

Of course, she was an expert at keeping people

at bay. Everyone knew she worked in the palace, but she never told them about her promotions up the ranks of the assistant pool to the point that she was now the king's personal assistant, albeit temporarily. She always told people the least she had to tell them to satisfy their curiosity because she didn't want her daughter's name to enter into things. She never knew when a tabloid or even legitimate press would start poking around, looking for her daughter for an update. So she was careful. And it didn't hurt. It didn't even matter. She loved her privacy.

As she took two cans of soup out of her shopping bag, her phone rang. Setting them on the counter, she turned to get her purse and picked up her phone to see the caller was her daughter.

She hit the screen to answer. "Speak of the devil."

Eleanore, now Ellie, said, "You were talking about me?"

"No. I was thinking how my lifestyle lends itself to privacy, which protects you…but also, how I like being alone." The temptation rose to tell her about the king—a guy she seemed to be able to talk to easily, if only because she and Ellie both had issues with men after being betrayed. But she remembered the almost kiss and the simple joy of it. Maybe she'd tell Eleanore after the assignment was over, when the conversation could be whimsical fun about what it was like to work for a king. After all, Mateo deserved his privacy too—

Darn it! She'd done it again. Thought of him as his first name rather than His Majesty.

"Honestly, that whole privacy thing is something I don't have to worry about here. I love Brazil."

"From what I've seen when I visited, I loved it too." With her phone on speaker, she took an apple out of a bag, rinsed it off to eat and said, "So what's up?"

"Nothing. Just checking in. Though I have to admit I did wonder why you were late getting home tonight. I've been calling since six o'clock."

Once again, the urge to tell Ellie about her new position and the gorgeous king stole through her. Like a schoolgirl who'd been noticed by the popular guy, she wanted to gush.

Ridiculous.

"Really? I never heard it ring. Plus, I had to stop at the store for groceries…" Not a lie, but the easy way she hedged the truth that she'd been inspecting a ballroom with a king made her realize how often she did that. She didn't have a boatload of friends, and those friends she did have didn't know everything about her. Only what they needed to know. Because she was an expert at keeping things to herself—which made it even more odd that she was so open with the king. *A king.* For God's sake. What was she doing getting close to this guy?

She got out of the conversation without talking about the waltz by promising herself she'd give Ellie every wonderful detail when the job was over. By the time her two months as his assistant were finished, she'd surely be beyond her unusual feelings around him. Familiarity bred contempt and while she didn't want to dislike him, it would be great not to want to swoon around him.

Saturday night, though, he crept into her thoughts again and she wondered what was going on at the ball. It might be his son's birthday party, but certain dignitaries had been invited. There would be unattached women all around Mateo, hitting on him because he was gorgeous and eligible. She wondered how he'd managed to stay single for the six years since his wife's death, then suddenly realized his daughter Sabrina would have been twelve when her mother died.

Though it was none of her business, thinking through Sabrina's situation was a smarter thing to ponder than Mateo's love life or lack thereof. Talking about his kids was a safe subject. Not just because it eased those times when her attraction was so tempting, but because he'd said he wanted help with his kids, meaning it was part of her job to see things he might not.

She tried to imagine how Ellie would have reacted if Jessica had died suddenly but the vision was distorted by her father's potential behavior. Would he have brought women to the house? Would he have cared for his daughter or ignored her? He probably would have ignored her. He was so self-centered that it sometimes floored her that she hadn't really understood it until he'd left their daughter twisting in the wind during the trial.

Luckily, Mateo wasn't like that. Extremely strong and powerful, he nonetheless had a sensitive side when it came to his kids.

She squeezed her eyes shut. Here she was again. Back to thinking about him. He might need her to step in or notice things, but she couldn't use that as an excuse to think about him all the time.

In fact, there was a novel on her bedside table that she should be reading. That was her point of contact with *her* future. She'd be gardening, reading, communing with nature. *That's* what she wanted.

The idyllic vision in her brain shimmied and shifted. She suddenly saw herself as an old crone with her hair in a bun and wrapped in a shawl, bent over her roses, someone with regrets because her life was incomplete.

She shook her head to get rid of the image. She'd been married, had a child, gone through a major life crisis with her daughter. Now she was working for a king. She'd seen and done plenty.

She had no reason for regrets or to think something was missing.

She read for two hours then went to bed reminding herself that she'd seen and done enough for one lifetime, which ushered in thoughts of Mateo again.

That was probably why she'd dreamed about him.

Monday morning, Jessica woke grouchy. She wasn't sure which bothered her the most: the fact that the wonderful future she'd imagined suddenly seemed quiet and made for a gnarled old woman, or the way she couldn't stop thinking about the *king* she was working for.

Annoyed with herself, she entered Mateo's quarters for their start-of-the-day meeting. She straightened her shoulders, forcing herself to be professional. She could not believe that the vision of the future that had kept her sane during the trial now seemed dull. Worse was the way her nerves jangled when she thought of Mateo dancing with women at the ball. She shouldn't care. She *didn't* care. That wasn't her. And from here on out she'd behave like her normal self. Not a wannabe Cinderella. Not a woman flummoxed by an unexpected attraction. But a worker bee. The king's assistant. The person who kept him on track and helped him run his life. The person he could count on.

That was who she was.

Period.

As she walked into the dining room, Mateo rose. "Good morning."

He looked magnificent in his dark suit and white shirt, definitely like one of the men who ruled the world. His good looks acknowledged, she let those thoughts slide away.

"Good morning." All business, she set her tablet on the table beside her plate. "You know, it dawned on me that with an official event being held in the palace, I probably should have asked if you wanted me to work the weekend."

He motioned for her to sit, as he lowered himself to his chair, just as he had every other morning.

"Actually, I spent Saturday and Sunday clearing up paperwork that didn't require your help. Honestly, if there is ever a reason why I need you on a non-workday, you will be called."

She nodded, closing the subject, very relieved their dealings were back to boss and assistant.

Nevil, the butler, brought two plates of eggs, bacon and fried potatoes and set one in front of each of them. She just looked at hers as Nevil walked away.

He winced. "I'm sorry. They're so accustomed to catering to me that they brought you the same thing I'm having."

"It's fine. I love bacon and eggs." She grimaced. "But I don't usually eat this much. I'm going to have to start skipping lunch."

"Or you could walk the grounds a couple times a day. Working in this part of the palace, you have access to my track."

Access to his track felt like a perk she didn't deserve, but maybe that was part of her problem? Instead of accepting the benefits of her assignment, she was making a big deal out of them—when they weren't. Technically, working for a king should come with some advantages. A track was a simple, harmless, wonderful thing.

"Thank you. I'll bring yoga pants and a T-shirt tomorrow."

"We also have a shower in the locker room."

Her skin prickled.

It shouldn't have. A shower in a locker room was ordinary, expected. Not an invitation. Not a chance to be around each other in various stages of undress. Her silly brain was going off the deep end again.

"Since you'll be here two months, we'll assign you a locker and you can put in whatever you need." He thought for a second, then added, "Given that you will have been in this part of the palace for months...I'll talk with HR about allowing you to keep it." He smiled at her. "As a thank-you of a sort for stepping in for Arthur."

"That's very kind of you."

He opened his napkin. She opened hers. They picked up their forks. Each dug into their breakfast.

The table got quiet and stayed quiet. After a few minutes, she wondered why he hadn't jumped into a discussion of his schedule. Normally, that was what he did.

She was just about to bring it up herself when he said, "Don't you want to ask about the ball?"

She desperately did, but she was working to suppress her interest because what she was most interested in was the ladies he'd danced with, the ones he'd spoken to. Opening that can of worms when her brain was finally on track seemed risky. "I'm sure you all had a great time."

"We did! It was spectacular." He leaned forward conspiratorially. His dark eyes brightened with joy, and she suddenly saw the reason it was so difficult to keep her own feelings in check. He was excited to tell her, to share with her.

They were kindred spirits.

"Some balls are more fun than others. My son's friends are a particularly happy group. They danced every song and groaned when the band took a break."

She let the kindred spirits idea sink in. It certainly explained why they'd gotten so close so quickly. "They do sound fun."

"I danced the first song with Sabrina to more or less open the dancing, then I did some schmoozing… There were people in attendance that I needed private time with."

She carefully met his gaze. "You worked?"

"Things like balls are great opportunities. Everybody's happy." His voice was matter-of-fact, confirming that what she sensed was correct. He didn't worry about confiding in her because he knew she would keep anything he said to herself. Even if she hadn't signed a confidentiality agreement, their conversations were private. "Everybody's in the mood to let bygones be bygones or maybe accept something they might have had reservations about."

She should have let the subject die, but the instinct to converse went both ways. He was such a nice guy, a good father, a determined leader that thinking about him working at a ball struck her as wrong. "So, you didn't have fun?"

"It was fun. It was great fun watching my son and his friends celebrate. And Sabrina was particularly well-behaved." He chuckled at what she was sure had to have been the look of concern on her face. "Being a king is not what everybody thinks it is. Especially if you're a *ruling* king."

She looked around the dining room of his quarters as if seeing it for the first time. All the while she'd been imagining him dancing and laughing with female guests, he'd been wheeling and dealing in dark corners.

He was right. Most people probably had no idea what it was like being a king. He was his job and his job was his life. She'd realized this before.

But knowing him a full week now, having had a peek behind the curtain, it took on new meaning.

She met his gaze again. "Do you ever have fun?"

The question rolled around in Mateo's brain for a few seconds. He could take his answer in a very personal direction and talk with someone who wouldn't judge. But she would be a part of his life for another seven weeks. It was more important for her to understand his work than for him to enjoy being able to speak freely with someone... to be himself.

He answered slowly, but truthfully. "It's as much fun for me to jump on diplomatic opportunities as it is to dance."

"You think striking a deal is fun?"

"Yes. I know my life is weird and honestly, it's good that you're seeing the truth of it. The more you see, the more you'll understand why I'm concerned about Sabrina's behavior. I don't want her to say or do something that could haunt her forever. But I'm also her dad. I worry that I missed teaching her something."

She nodded.

Seeing the concern in her eyes, he sighed. "The way our private lives and work lives intertwine seems like an albatross but it's also a privilege. It doesn't make sense until you understand how much of an honor it is to be charged with keeping our people employed, safe, happy. I'm failing at finding the way to help Sabrina understand that."

He waited a few seconds while Jessica absorbed what he'd said.

He wasn't surprised when she spoke openly with him. "I don't think you give yourself enough credit. Even with a spouse and a normal life, I had some issues raising my daughter. I can't imagine how you do it, as a royal…and alone. When my husband backed out of Ellie's situation, I got a taste of being a single parent. It's not easy."

Her understanding and grasp of his life was like a soothing balm. Not that he needed anyone's approval or for anyone to really comprehend what his life had been like. But having her understand his fears about raising Sabrina meant something. And though he knew it was wrong, he let himself enjoy it.

Jessica continued on. "Kids in middle school can be mean. Kids in high school are always trying things. Ellie wanted to go to an American beach for spring break her final year of secondary school. We didn't let her go but when she was at university, she didn't need our permission…"

She stopped.

His heart thudded. She'd accidentally stepped into the story of when her daughter had been drugged. Just as he found it so easy to talk to her, it seemed she also let her guard down enough with him that something she undoubtedly wanted to keep private had slipped out.

The room stilled, the air filled with anticipation. Of what, he wasn't sure. He didn't think she'd intended to tell him about her daughter's situation, but now that she had opened the door, he wished she would trust him.

When a full minute of silence went by, he decided to give her a nudge, hoping she'd open up.

"You blame yourself for what happened to your daughter?"

She sucked in a breath and carefully said, "We should have at least tried to stop her. Not been so accepting."

The butler came in with a fresh pot of coffee, Joshua on his heels.

"Good morning!" Always cheerful at the start of the day, Mateo's son took a seat at the dining room table. "Ah. Bacon."

"Jessica, this is my son Joshua. Joshua, this is Jessica Smith, Arthur's temporary replacement."

"Nice to meet you. Am I here in time for the review of the schedule?"

"We didn't get to it yet," Mateo said. He faced Jessica. While he battled disappointment that such an important conversation had been abruptly ended, she seemed relieved.

She picked up her tablet. Joshua told Nevil he'd have the same breakfast the king was having. As Nevil scurried out, Jessica began listing his appointments for the day. The meal went on like business as usual.

But he couldn't stop thinking about Jessica and her daughter. He didn't merely want to hear the story. He knew she needed to talk about it. The same way he longed to talk with someone who would understand, not judge, she needed someone in the public eye, someone who'd faced down the press and his critics, to understand her.

But that would mean creating a true confidence. The things she saw in his palace, the things she overheard, the things he would tell her might have national security implications. Her keeping that information to herself was a part of her job.

Her story was of a broken heart. Getting her to tell him that story created a connection. A genuine, personal connection—

Longing for exactly that rippled through him.

Still, as much as it tempted him… Was it the right thing to do? She was a temporary employee. He was ruler of a kingdom, a man who out of necessity put his country before himself. He wasn't supposed to get close to an employee.

Somedays, he genuinely believed he wasn't supposed to be close to anyone.

That usually didn't bother him, but today it seemed wrong. Or maybe off-sync. As if he'd misinterpreted his entire life.

And in a way, Jessica paid the price because he

sensed more than ever that he should return the favor and let her get her story off her chest.

To tell him—someone who really would understand.

And he couldn't let her.

CHAPTER FIVE

DISCUSSING A BORING trade agreement most of the morning, Mateo let his gaze drift to the door between his office and Jessica's. If he wanted to know the details of her daughter's troubles, he could probably find everything somewhere on the internet. But information wasn't what stole his focus.

It haunted him that Jessica was so hard on herself. He tried to imagine how he would feel if someone drugged Olivia or Sabrina and the desire for blood swelled in him as a hot wave.

The dignitary left and as Mateo ate lunch, he pulled out his phone. He searched Eleanore Smith—not Ellie. He'd noticed Jessica had used a shortened version of her name and knew that was because Eleanore Smith was immediately recognizable. Article after article popped up. He didn't read the text, only studied the pictures.

Eleanore walking into the courthouse with Jessica by her side.

Eleanore in the courtroom at the politician's trial, her mother sitting beside her.

Jessica was in every picture. Except her name was Pennelope. Pennelope Smith. The Smith might be common, but Pennelope wasn't. Just like her daughter, she now used another name to at least give herself a modicum of privacy.

The more important thing, though, was that she'd never left her daughter's side.

He returned to his office to find Jessica wasn't at her desk. Before he had a chance to question that, his office door opened. Pete walked in with billionaire CEO Allen Risk.

Risk extended his hand to shake Mateo's. "Thank you for seeing me, Your Majesty."

"It's my pleasure." He motioned for Allen Risk to sit on the chair kitty-corner to his comfortable sofa. "I understand you want to set up shop in Pocetak."

Tall, slender, confident, Allen grinned. "Yes."

"To do what exactly?" The billionaire had only gotten an audience because he was well-known for being on the cutting edge of technology. The right project could shift Pocetak from mediocracy to relevance in the next decade.

"I want a space program."

Positive he'd heard wrong, Mateo laughed. "What?"

"The US has NASA and Elon Musk. There's no room for me."

"And you think there is here?"

Allen sat forward, putting his forearms on his

knees and caught Mateo's gaze as if confiding. "Picture it. Long-distance travel using space. A trip to Australia would be a few hours. Japan would be a hop, skip and a jump." He grinned again. "Let me set up here, and I'll employ some of your best and brightest who might not feel like they have opportunities in your current labor pool. I'll need everything from lawyers and engineers to blue-collar workers for assembly. Plus, your country will get a name for being on the forefront of the involved technologies."

And his best and brightest would have reason to stay in Mateo's country. Allen didn't have to say it. They both knew people with advanced degrees weren't afraid to relocate, some even leaving their countries for greener pastures.

He sat back. "I'd be willing to see a prospectus. At least a ten-year plan."

Allen sniffed. "How about a five-year plan?"

Mateo smiled. "I want ten. I want to see that you won't come in here and get everyone all excited and then desert us."

He sat back. "I'm committed."

Mateo rose. "Good. Then it should be easy for you to write a ten-year plan."

Allen rolled his eyes but rose too. "I want to know that you are more than considering this."

"Having you run that kind of program here would be a boon to our economy and our people in general. We're solid. We're not going anywhere.

You're the wild card. I look forward to you showing us that you're serious and committed."

Allen held out his hand for shaking. Grinning again, his self-confidence back full force, he said, "Okay."

He left through the office door and within seconds Jessica walked in. He had no idea how she knew Allen had gone, but she'd popped in at exactly the right time.

"You have two more appointments. Molly's sending General Wojak down now," she said without looking at him. "This is just a briefing before the big meeting you have tomorrow with the heads of all branches of the military. The second meeting is with a union rep looking for your support. Files for that are on your desk."

She said it efficiently and turned to walk out of his office.

A weird feeling shuffled through him. She needed to talk and he was probably exactly the kind of person she needed to talk to, but he was holding back. He simply didn't think it wise to cross that line with an employee.

But while the general went on for an hour about border control and two treaties that were expiring, Mateo thought about Jessica, knowing her cool efficiency was either the result of her not wanting to discuss her daughter or the guilt she'd inadvertently admitted.

He decided it was the guilt. The upset about unintentionally mentioning her daughter would have easily melted away because Joshua's appearance stopped the conversation from going any further than a few sentences. So it couldn't be that. It had to be guilt.

He could talk to her about guilt...couldn't he?

The general left. Ten minutes later, the union guy entered.

Mateo always knew that his life was busy, but back-to-back meetings were killing him that day. With the hours that had gone by, he now knew he didn't want Jessica to bare her soul. He simply wanted to tell her that she shouldn't feel guilty, and talking about that was not a big deal. It was not the start of an inappropriate personal relationship. It was simply finishing a conversation. Letting her know he understood. One human being to another.

Unfortunately, the union rep talked for hours.

When he finally left, Jessica walked into Mateo's office. "Are there notes or anything you want to dictate for me to type up?"

"No. I make notes on my tablet, then beef them up myself. It's my way of reviewing the meeting." He paused, getting ready to shift the discussion back to where it had been at breakfast before Joshua arrived.

But she quickly said, "Thank you, Your Majesty," turned and headed out the door. "Good night."

All right. That was a sign. A signal. She did not want to talk about her daughter with him.

Which was probably for the best.

He glanced at his watch, saw it was after seven o'clock, and realized why she'd gone so quickly. Discomfort rumbled through him. He kept her late on a day when she probably wanted to get home and forget everything she'd said—

Maybe. But he couldn't get rid of the awful itchy feeling that they needed to finish that conversation. That she needed to talk, or he needed to help her to see that she shouldn't feel guilty. *Something.*

He ate dinner with Sabrina and Olivia, but as soon as the girls left, he called the motor pool. Ten minutes later, he was in a car and headed for town.

He'd changed clothes and now wore jeans and a nondescript shirt. He also had a cap pulled down over his forehead, more or less altering the look of his face. Plus, it was a bit after nine. Only a smattering of people still milled on the streets. Most of them were probably headed home.

When they neared her building, he leaned forward and spoke to the driver. "Pull over and let me out here." They'd taken a black sedan, not a limo, but he still didn't want the car to stop in front of her home.

"Yes, sire." His driver frowned. "But are you sure?"

"We're a block away. I'll be fine. My detail is

only a few feet behind us. They've been instructed to blend in, but they are there."

Shoulders hunched and head down, he walked to her building. He opened the door and looked for an elevator. There was none. He wasn't sure if he should gripe or laugh. Luckily, he jogged every day, and four flights of steps was simply additional cardio.

When a knock sounded on her door, Jessica's head snapped up. She never got visitors—especially not this late—but if someone from the building needed something, she liked being a friendly neighbor. She jumped up and walked to the door, taking a second to look through the peephole.

Seeing the king dressed like a normal guy, she yanked open the door.

"What are you doing?" She grabbed his arm and pulled him inside her small apartment.

He shoved his hands in his jean pockets. The sight of him, looking so normal, sent jolts of confusion and attraction through her.

The man knew how to wear a pair of jeans.

"I...um...felt uncomfortable with the way we left our discussion at breakfast when Joshua joined us. We never finished it."

He took in her oversize T-shirt and black yoga pants, then her bare feet, looking at her the way a man looks at a woman, not like a king. Just a guy.

Her nerve endings sparked to life. She couldn't

believe she'd made that slip about Ellie. But having him worry about her—enough that he had put on jeans and a knit cap and sneaked out of the palace to check on her—sent the warmth of pleasure spiraling through her, even as the kindness of it touched her heart.

Still, this was a king. The conversation had started because he had been concerned about his own child. Telling him about her situation with Ellie had been a way to show him that all parents second-guessed themselves, but she'd gone on too long. She'd actually been glad they were interrupted.

"That's because the conversation was over."

"But you blame yourself for what happened to your daughter."

She took a breath, then walked over to the sofa to move her book so she could offer him a seat. But really, she needed a minute. Not one other person in her life had noticed that she blamed herself. Nobody else had ever cared. Of course, she was secretive with everyone—

Except him. Her openness with him was so uncharacteristic that it scared her. She liked this job. She *needed* this job. And allowing things to get personal could ruin that. Worse, it was wrong for her to get involved with a king. Any boss for that matter. But a king was someone of note and reputation and recognition. She shouldn't burden him with her life.

Unfortunately, she could also see from the look on his face as he sat on her comfortable, but worn sofa, that he wasn't going to let her pretend everything was fine.

She sat on the chair across from him. "Yes, I blame myself…" She could admit that because he clearly saw it. Now, she would steer him away from worry. "But millions of kids go on vacation alone without incident. She was twenty. Old enough to make her own choices. I have come to terms with that."

"Not if you still blame yourself."

She took a breath and looked at the ceiling. "All right. Sometimes I wonder if there was something I missed teaching her. Then I remind myself that all she had to do was turn her head away from her drink for two seconds for someone to drop some powder into it."

"So, what bothers you, then, is just that it happened."

"That Ellie was the unlucky woman in the wrong place at the wrong time with the wrong person?" She shrugged. "Something like that. The arbitrariness of it. In a way, no one is safe."

"That's not really a good way to live your life." He looked around. "Is that why you're here? In an apartment? Because no one would expect you to be here? Your ex was a well-known lawyer. I'm sure your divorce settlement would have allowed you to afford more than this."

She didn't question his knowledge of her finances. She was sure HR thoroughly vetted her before she was hired.

Instead, she laughed. "Are you calling my apartment a dive?"

"Not a dive as much as a hidden place."

"That's part of it, but it's more about saving for retirement."

His eyes narrowed. "Seriously? You're living simply so you can save for retirement?"

Glad for the shift of topic, she said, "I want to retire early. I envision myself buying a really cute cottage in the country, and gardening and reading."

He shook his head. "Wow. You really do want to check out, don't you?"

"Check out?"

"Live separate. Ignore the world."

Of course she did. She'd learned a lot about people during her daughter's trial. But she wouldn't tell him that. He still seemed to be worried about her. And he needn't be. She was very good at taking care of herself.

"Nope. Just saving for retirement."

"Humph. Retirement." He pondered that. "It's something I've never considered."

"You have responsibilities."

"Big ones," he agreed. "I'm the person who keeps war at bay so you can retire in your cottage and forget the rest of us exist."

She laughed again then inclined her head slightly in acceptance of that. "Thank you."

"Are you kidding me? That's all I get? Thanks for keeping the world safe so you can check out." He rolled his eyes. "I came here because I was worried about you but you're very comfortably hiding."

"I wouldn't say I was hiding."

"Oh, you are hiding."

"It's not a sin."

"No. It's not. It's just not a luxury afforded to all of us."

She gaped at him. "Are you jealous?"

"Maybe a little."

She laughed. "Come on. Don't pout."

"I'm not pouting. Just thinking things through."

She rose from the chair and sat beside him on the sofa, bridging the physical distance between them as a way to sort of comfort him. "I'd trade places with you any day of the week."

He snorted. "No, you wouldn't."

"All right. I wouldn't. But can we just agree that both of our lives come with some quirks and restrictions?"

He took a breath. "Yes." His voice softened. "But I don't like thinking of you as guilt-ridden."

She smiled. "I'm not. I helped Ellie recover by teaching her to focus on the future. Because that was what helped me. All through the trial, I pondered what our future would hold and how our lives needed to change so that when the trial was over, we were ready." She motioned around the room. "Believe it or not, living like this, saving, makes my future seem real."

He studied her eyes. "You're a remarkable woman."

Mesmerized by his soft voice, she suddenly realized how close they were sitting. But she didn't move. "Don't give me too much credit. It was a learn-as-you-go situation."

He leaned toward her, whispering. "And it looks like you aced it."

Their gazes caught and clung. Her voice soft as a feather, she said, "I did."

Once again, they were close enough to kiss. This time she wasn't letting her brain tell her that anticipation was better than the actual kiss. She wanted the kiss. He did too or he would have moved away.

Still, she wouldn't make the move. He had to do it.

He negated the final few inches between them, his lips touching hers ever so slightly. When she didn't protest, he caught her upper arms to pull her closer and kissed her completely.

Everything inside her shimmered. Curiosity and need tightened her chest. His soft lips applied just enough pressure to send tingles of delight through her. But it was closeness, the rightness that made it perfect. Kissing him was like coming home. She'd dated a few men since her divorce but hadn't ever felt this. Actually, she'd never even felt this for her ex.

She stretched forward the slightest bit. He deepened the kiss. Even as she clung to the reality that reminded her that she did not want this particular fairy tale, she let herself fall into it. Allowed herself to feel all the sensations of being kissed and held. Somehow his arms had gone around her, and a warm, protected feeling enveloped her. Not because he was kissing her, but because he wanted to kiss her. The same way she wanted to kiss him. It was a powerful, tempting thought.

He eased back, stared into her eyes for a few seconds, then said, "That was amazing."

She whispered, "I know."

He took a breath, pulled his arms away from her and rose from the sofa. "I should…" He rubbed his hand across the back of his neck. "I should go. But I'm not sorry I came. I just couldn't get that conversation out of my head. I needed to know you were okay. Really okay with everything. Not just okay with the fact that you slipped an important piece of information to me."

She rose too, slowly. The impulsiveness of kissing had been unexpected, but wonderful.

"I've made mistakes with my kids, blamed myself because I'm the parent who is supposed to be guiding them, but your situation is different." He sighed. "As you said, arbitrary. There was something inside me that rebelled at thinking you blamed yourself for the actions of someone who was the dregs of society."

She sniffed. "Well, now he's got a prison number, so we at least get the satisfaction of knowing he couldn't fool anyone else."

He took a step closer. "That's really the bottom line, isn't it? That he might have been doing this for a while, but someone finally stopped him."

"That was Eleanore's crusade. What kept her strong. The knowledge that if she pushed through this and he was convicted, she wasn't a victim anymore but a fighter. Not a crusader. Simply someone who was wronged and she got justice."

"That's a very good way to look at it."

She nodded. "Yes."

"So, no more guilt?"

"I'll probably forever have my moments when I say I wish I had argued, stopped her, been there…"

He slid his hand to the curve of her jaw. "But?"

She swallowed. He was going to kiss her again. They both knew it. Even after pulling away and standing up, intending to leave, they'd extended the conversation just long enough that he seemed to have forgotten he shouldn't have kissed her—

Why the hell did this all feel so right?

"But I promise. I will now banish those thoughts and remind myself that she is strong and smart."

"Like her mother."

His whispered words danced on her skin. A

compliment to be sure, but a connection. He saw her. The real her. While everyone else saw a good worker, a quiet but reliable neighbor, he saw *her*. That's why all this felt so right. She'd already realized they were kindred spirits, but right now they were tiptoeing toward destiny.

He slid his hands to her shoulders and bent his head. He paused right before their lips would meet, holding her gaze, giving her a chance to stop him. She didn't. As much as her heart was thinking foolish things like destiny, her brain knew there was no such thing as people who were meant to be together. Everyone's life was a series of actions, reactions and decisions. Things that tumbled into each other. When he returned home, to his palace, he would look around and realize nothing could come of the feelings they had for each other, and he would decide that a couple kisses was all the destiny they would get.

Which was all the more reason to enjoy what would probably be their final kiss.

Their lips met softly again, but this time she decided to be the aggressor. She touched his lips with her tongue and the floodgates of need opened. He pulled her close and she wrapped her arms around his neck as the kiss went on and on, warm and delicious.

Once again, he pulled back. His hands slid from her biceps, down her forearms to her fingertips before he finally broke contact.

Regret filled the air. It was the poignant end of anything personal between them. The next morning, he would be a working king, someone who carried the weight of his little corner of the world on his shoulders, and she would be the assistant who helped him reach his goals.

Nothing more.

"I'll see you in the morning."

Emptiness filled her. "See you in the morning."

Walking to her door, he retrieved the knit cap from his pocket and smoothed it on his head, reminding her of the great lengths he'd gone to to see her.

Her breath caught, but she remembered the way he'd eased away from her. The finality of it.

He opened the door and left.

And that was the end of her fairy tale.

Because the very thing that brought him to her that night, his worry about her past, was the thing that destroyed even a wisp of hope they could follow what they felt. The press would love to find her with a king. Not only would they salivate over the sensational stories they could print—

But her daughter would be exposed again.

She would never deliberately do anything that would hurt her daughter.

CHAPTER SIX

THE NEXT MORNING Jessica arrived in the dining room for breakfast, wearing her professional face. He would have laughed, except all this was very serious. For as much as it might cause turmoil in *his* life if the press discovered their interest in each other, it would cause a hundred times more problems for her.

Not to mention troubles for her daughter. A story that had been closed for years would be re-opened, along with the old wounds that accompanied it.

He needed to assure her that she had nothing to worry about. He wouldn't ever again show up at her apartment uninvited. He wouldn't pursue her. He'd tried to say that the night before, but he'd been so gobsmacked by their kiss that he'd given mixed messages.

He would rectify that now.

"Good morning, Ms. Smith."

She set her tablet on the table. "Good morning, Your Majesty."

Joshua and Olivia picked that exact second to enter the dining room. "I'm telling you that he's not the innocent you think he is."

Both walked to the table. Olivia smiled and said, "Jessica Smith, right? We never got a chance to meet but I'm Olivia…" She bobbed her head and grinned. "The one who will take over when Dad decides to retire."

"She's such a braggart," Joshua said, pulling out his chair.

"You're just jealous because it's not you."

He snorted. "It's no great feat to be born first. You had nothing to do with it. So don't act like it's an accomplishment."

"It will be an accomplishment if she can handle the job," Mateo said. He wasn't happy his kids had shown up. But it was good for Olivia to meet Jessica. "And I'm sorry you haven't yet met Ms. Smith. She'll be doing everything Arthur did."

Olivia brightened. "Oh, I hope you tossed out those old notes he had about what Dad should wear to certain events." She grimaced and shuddered. "I swear I want to burn that one military uniform."

He sighed. "It's tradition. Like it or not, you'll be following those same rules, or the press will want to know why."

The mention of the press gave him a squeezy feeling and his gaze shot to Jessica. She immediately looked down at her coffee cup, which Nevil was currently filling.

Nevil moved to pour Olivia's coffee, and she said, "You haven't seen me because last week wasn't my week to meet with Dad. This week is." She smiled at Nevil as he shifted away. "It's not like we have actual meetings where he explains how to rule. But we do deconstruct some of the things happening in parliament."

Jessica smiled at his daughter. "Right now, you're serving in parliament, right?"

Olivia angled her thumb at Joshua. "Under *him*."

"Because he's second in command in parliament," Mateo said to Jessica. "He won't take over completely until he's twenty-five."

"And done with school," Joshua said. "If Dad reigns another twenty years that's a lot of years that I get to torment her before she's my boss."

Olivia rolled her eyes. "You'd best remember that because if you push too far, I'll have a hundred ways to get revenge."

The teasing continued as Nevil took breakfast orders. When he left, the conversation shifted to actual business. Jessica quietly took in what was being said, but Mateo could also see her absorbing the family dynamic. She would be the perfect replacement for Arthur if he ever decided to retire. She was good at her job, but she also knew how to move from his professional life to his personal life and back again without so much as hiccup.

Which was another reason to get time alone with her to have that discussion where he would very clearly promise her that he wouldn't upend her life by pursuing her. Arthur had never before asked for a leave of absence and Mateo had to consider that he was testing out the idea of retiring. If he decided it was time, Jessica would be the perfect replacement. Telling her that would prove his desire to keep their relationship professional.

When their food was served, Jessica activated her tablet and began the discussion of his schedule. Olivia and Joshua paid close attention. They might love to squabble and tease, but they were both dedicated leaders. No matter what Joshua said, he was committed to their country and his sister. Plus, he liked being next in line to head parliament. It was hands-on politics and he was good at it.

They were going to be an amazing team.

Jessica made entries on his schedule as his children added events to his calendar, then she left to get things organized. He walked up to her desk twenty minutes later.

"Jessica, could you come into my office for a few minutes?"

Grabbing her tablet, she said, "Absolutely."

He would take the first five minutes to give her his reassurances, then that would be out of the way, and they could get down to work.

But before they even sat down, Pete arrived

with one of the two union representatives from the day before.

He just looked at them. "George?"

George walked into the office, his hand extended for shaking. "It's our regular meeting the morning after the meeting." When Mateo was certain he must have looked confused, George added, "We always meet the day after talking with all the representatives so I can clear things up—explain how we came to certain decisions. That kind of thing."

Jessica scrambled for her tablet again, hitting the screen a few times.

She peeked up. "You're not on the schedule."

"I'm never 'on the schedule.' It's not a secret meeting, but it's not something we want advertised."

She turned to Mateo apologetically. "I should have realized an hour of blank space on your calendar meant something. I take full responsibility."

He motioned for George to have a seat. "No harm done, Ms. Smith."

She nodded and left the room from the right, as Pete exited from the main office door.

George took a seat. Kitchen staff brought in coffee. He and George talked for an hour and then Pete brought in a group of kids who'd won that year's Geography Bee for pictures. George said his goodbyes and left.

A huge encourager of education, Mateo posed

with the group, then each one individually. As he gave them a short talk on the value of learning and hinted that great opportunities might be coming to their country and they needed to be ready, Pete watched over the scene like a proud papa. When Mateo stopped talking, Pete herded the kids out. Even before Mateo could get organized enough to call Jessica in, Pete returned with a stack of documents.

"I'm leaving at noon," he explained with his usual sunny smile. "Dentist. Otherwise, I would have waited until three o'clock to bring these in."

Mateo nodded, sitting at his desk in front of the big stack he would be expected to read before he signed.

He took a breath, as Pete left his office, then paged Jessica who arrived with her tablet. She eyed the big stack of correspondence and reports.

"What are your plans for lunch?"

"I have none," she said, still taking in the big stack of papers. "If you need help with that," she said, and nudged her head toward the documents on his desk, "we can get started now."

"Oh, I'm going to need help with that, but we'll tackle it this afternoon. I want to steal a few minutes alone for one final discussion between us."

She caught his gaze. "I thought we didn't have anything to talk about."

"Just maybe some reassurances."

Though she looked like she wanted to argue, she said, "I'll meet you in the dining room."

"Actually, let's meet in the stables."

She frowned and glanced down at her dress.

"Did you bring things for your locker as I suggested?"

She nodded.

"Hopefully, you'll have trousers in there."

"How about yoga pants?"

"Good enough. And you ride?"

She winced. "A little."

He smiled. "You'll be fine. We'll get you the gentlest horse."

A few minutes before noon, she strode into the stables, wearing yoga pants and a sweatshirt. He smiled when he saw her, but she grimaced. "I don't run the track in finery."

"No one does." He displayed a picnic basket, and she realized the stables were empty. No one would see the basket or realize they were going out riding together. She didn't know if that was because it was normal for the stable to be empty at lunchtime or if he had arranged this. But either way, no one saw them.

"Are we ready?"

Remembering just how long it had been since she'd been on a horse, she said, "I hope so."

As promised, the stable staff had provided her with an extremely gentle, smaller-than-average horse. She remembered how to mount and within seconds they were easing out of the stable.

They rode slowly through a huge, slightly sloped grassy area with just enough trees to provide a bit of cover, until they came to a fence. He opened a hidden gate, and they continued on through tall grass that swayed in the almost-May breeze.

She glanced around in awe. The palace was now so far back it was growing smaller and smaller. "How big is this estate?"

"A thousand acres."

She gaped at him. "We're going to ride a thousand acres?"

"No. We're actually on the short side of the property. There's a lot more land to the left of the palace. But either way, we keep the land extremely private. There are four fences. The very edge of the property doesn't have a fence, so no one realizes it's royal land. It just looks like a grassy field. The area borders a forest where people regularly hike, so the trees on the edge are peppered with hidden cameras and motion detectors. Nothing happens if someone accidentally steps into our land. Especially if they simply leave."

"Everything they do is recorded?"

"Everything they do on *royal land* is recorded. The first fence is actually fairly far into the property, at another strip of trees. There is nothing about it that says this is royal land. It's just a wooden fence. Again, that area is monitored with cameras. On the other side of those trees is another fence with sporadic cameras." He motioned beyond them to the grassy area. "That's where we're going."

"So there are two fences and hundreds of cameras beyond that grassy area?"

He winced. "I wouldn't say hundreds."

"Wow. You really do want privacy, don't you?"

"Do you want someone to see us?"

She thought about her life and his life and Ellie's somewhat quiet life and said, "Oh, my goodness. No."

"I never realized how congested my schedule is until this week." He snorted. "Then, today, trying to get two minutes alone with you?" He shook his head. "We had to come out here to get even thirty seconds of peace and privacy."

"On the bright side, you brought lunch."

He laughed. "That's what I like about you. You find the good in everything."

"Ellie's troubles made me an expert that that."

"Well, it's a good trait. Don't lose it."

He stopped his horse in a small cove of trees and dismounted.

She stopped hers. Then she frowned. "I forget how to get down."

He laughed and walked over. "Bring your right leg across the horse, and turn toward me."

She did. He caught her by the waist and swung her to the grassy field.

Batting her eyelashes, she purred at him. "Oh, you're so strong."

He rolled his eyes. "Stop. Even pretend flirting has to be off the table."

Though she agreed, she said nothing, glancing around, as he removed the picnic hamper from his horse and dug out a blanket.

"It's really nice out here."

"This is that privacy you're saving up for."

She looked around again. "Hey! It is!"

He motioned for her to sit on the blanket and pulled a few containers from the hamper. "Just sandwiches. I didn't want the staff to start wondering."

"Good plan." She took the sandwich he offered her, unwrapped it and took a bite. "Mmmm. Good."

"Our kitchen staff is the best."

"I still remember the blueberry pancakes." She waited a second, then said, "So why are we out here?"

He took a second. Once again, when he was alone with her, everything got confused. Or slowed down. Or something. He didn't feel the weight of his obligations. He didn't feel happy or sad or have a sense of expectation. He just felt comfortable. And that in and of itself was like a gift from heaven.

"My original intent had been to get a few minutes alone so that I could reassure you that the kisses from the night before were the end of my confusion about our relationship."

One of her eyebrows rose. "Original intent?"

He looked around, absorbing the peace and quiet of the area. "It was a busy morning. It's kind of nice being out here. Not thinking. Not doing. Just being. I want to soak that in for a minute before we have a depressing conversation."

"You know what's happening, don't you? You're seeing my point about the cottage in the woods."

He snorted. "Maybe, but, honestly, sitting on a blanket, outside in the fresh air, everything feels different."

"You're relaxed."

"No." He sucked in a breath. "I haven't figured it all out yet, but I think it has more to do with being alone with you."

"We're crossing over into that wrong territory again."

He motioned around them. "But it's okay. No one can see us."

"No cameras?"

"Not here." He smirked. "I checked." He pointed behind them. "Plus, see that fence back there."

She nodded.

"It's razor wire."

"What!"

"Don't worry. It's marked. And by the time anyone gets to that fence, all those cameras I told you about would have alerted staff, and they'd be there to greet the intruder before they got any further. But if they don't get here before the intruder, that wire's hard to climb or cut, trying to do either one keeps them at the fence long enough for my people to get out here, guns drawn."

"Now, I think you're just showing off."

"Give me that today. I don't get a chance to show off because people think it comes across as arrogant."

She chuckled.

"Seriously, I did want peace and quiet to tell you that I will behave. Watching you with Olivia and Josh this morning, I realized you'd be a perfect replacement for Arthur if he's testing out retirement in this leave of absence."

Her breath caught. "I would love that. Thank you."

"But the behaving doesn't start till we get back to the palace."

She looked at him.

"Come on. It's a beautiful day. We are totally alone. And this is it for us. Our last chance to just be us."

"You said that last night."

"It's not polite to argue with your king."

Her sandwich gone, she stuffed the wrapping into the hamper.

He finished his sandwich and stretched out on

his side, his elbow supporting his upper body, his head resting on his closed fist.

"Being drawn to someone like I am to you has never happened to me before."

"You've never been in love?"

"My marriage was arranged."

"So, you've never had that feeling of free-falling down a well?"

He laughed. "That does not sound fun."

"Honestly? At first, falling in love is kind of confusing. My ex was a partner at a law firm where I worked. He was handsome. He was smart. He was funny. When I realized he was interested in me, everything seemed to happen at once. It was confusing and out of control. Maybe chaotic is the best word. And yeah. I felt like I was falling."

Distaste filled him. "Falling for *him?*" The husband who'd deserted her and her daughter. The very idea was revolting.

"Yes. But it was smoke and mirrors. He wasn't the guy he pretended to be. After we were married, I started noticing little things, like how his needs always came first. But because we lived an extremely comfortable life, that didn't matter. I could always work around it. Then Ellie was raped, and he reacted weirdly."

"He wanted to kill the guy?"

"No. It was more that he saw the whole thing as an inconvenience."

Confused, he stared at her. "What?"

"Her trip, the aftermath, the trial…that was about three years. At first, he pretended to be a concerned parent. Then he got angry that it was interfering in his life. Though he didn't come right out and say it, I recognized the signs. Then one day, toward the end of the trial, he out-and-out belittled our daughter when a reporter asked him for a comment."

"What did he say?"

"He said this is nonsense and he wanted it over."

"Could it have just been a bad day?"

She shook her head. "Nope. He really was angry that Ellie wanted justice. He thought she should suck it up and get on with her life."

"That's when you left him."

"I kicked him out that night after a blowout argument."

"And you had another day in court the next morning."

"Yeah. I stood by Ellie, and he happily let us go alone."

"So, that love feeling you had didn't pan out?"

"It didn't. I mean I loved him, but maybe blindly. I should have seen sooner that he wasn't who he pretended to be. While I was free-falling, he was just fulfilling his life plan. I was like item number seven: Find a good woman and marry her." She paused a second, then said, "What about you? You never got the sense of free-falling with your wife? Not even after having kids? Or one Christmas morning?"

"My wife didn't want that."

"Really?"

"Like your husband, she didn't want to be bothered with anything she believed was beyond the scope of what she perceived her job as my wife to be. She did her duties with children and public appearances—oh, she loved public appearances. And she made it look like we were a happy couple."

"Weren't you?"

"We were a team. Not a couple. And, honestly, I was raised to believe that was a good thing. I wasn't disappointed in her. I wasn't disappointed in our marriage. I thought that was the way things should be. But as the kids got older, I saw that she didn't like being part of their lives."

Her face fell, as if what he'd said was incomprehensible. "Really? She didn't like being a mom?"

"I don't think so. I mean, she loved the kids. She just wanted them to be self-sufficient. When Sabrina turned ten, she started going on long trips with friends. I don't believe she was ever unfaithful, but she loved Fashion Week and film festivals and safaris...anything to get out of the palace and away from the kids."

She stared at him. "That's weird."

"No. It was very telling. She liked the person she had been, the life she'd had, before we were married and once the kids hit a certain age where she believed her work was done, she drifted back to that life."

"That was hard on you?"

"It was hard on the kids, which made it hard on me. I had no illusions about her. But I hated watching the kids lose theirs. I hated that there was an emptiness in their lives. I worked double time, loving them, doing things like movie nights and going on vacations as a family, while technically she left us. Until she got sick, then she came back. Used us again for a state funeral."

"Wow. She really soured you on marriage."

"Like your husband didn't sour you?"

"Oh, he did. I might date but it would be a cold frosty day in hell before I got married again." She leaned back on her elbows, stretching her legs in front of her. "Don't you think enough time's gone by that someone's going to miss us?"

"I've been watching. I'd say we have another fifteen minutes. Then I'll let you go back to the stables before me. I'll wait a half hour and dare anyone to ask me where I've been when I get back from lunch late."

She laughed, the sound drifted away on the breeze.

The romance of it rippled through him. Peace. Quiet. Privacy. With someone he liked very much.

"You know, everyone would love it if we'd start

dating. They'd love a royal romance. Widowed king smitten."

Obviously confused at the change of subject, she peered at him, but answered honestly. "They might love it if you started dating, but no one would want you dating me."

"Oh, it would be great until they dug into your past. But it wouldn't hurt me as much as it would hurt you…and your daughter." He shook his head. "But right now, none of that matters. No one knows. No one is digging for anything. We could come out here every day and no one would even suspect if we found a way to get out here separately. We couldn't use the stables every day—" He let the thought hang in the air, not sure where his brain was going.

"Are you suggesting that we regularly sneak onto the one part of your property that doesn't have a camera?"

She laughed, but he sat up, his thoughts coalescing. "We are sort of the perfect candidates for an affair. You have to be careful to protect your daughter's privacy. And I'm too much in the public eye for you to get involved with me." He motioned around again. "Yet here we are. Perfectly happy, almost giddy, because we like being together."

She grimaced. "Someone would figure it out."

He leaned back again, stopping his rushing thoughts before the idea could go any further.

Technically, he'd known her a little over a week. He shouldn't even be thinking about an affair, let alone suggesting one. The intensity of his feelings around her baffled him, until he thought about her description of falling in love. The confusion. The chaos.

But falling in love was an even worse idea than an affair.

Whatever was happening, he needed to stop it. Not just for his own sanity but for hers.

"You're right. Nothing ever stays a secret."

She rose. "What do you say? Is it time for me to go back to the stables?"

He sucked in a long breath then got to his feet. "Do you know the way?"

"It was pretty much a straight line."

He shoved his hands in his jeans pockets and glanced around. "Yeah."

Even he heard the disappointment in his voice. She walked over and pressed her hands to his chest before she rose to her tiptoes and kissed him. "My King Charming and I can't even keep you."

The way she'd so casually kissed him sent arousal fluttering through him. He bent and kissed her back. The arousal ramped up exponentially. He'd gone from conspiring romantic to desperate lover in about twenty seconds. Because she was right. She could not keep him. He couldn't keep her.

He broke the kiss, stepping back.

"I'll see you in the office."

She smiled and inched away from him. Then she turned and walked to her horse, which she mounted with only slight difficulty. In another ride or two, she'd be skilled at getting on and off the horse.

But there'd be no more rides, and he would suggest she be seen on the track tomorrow at lunch, so no one started questioning where she might have been on her lunch hour today.

Because as wonderful as an affair sounded, even that came with problems.

CHAPTER SEVEN

THE FOLLOWING MONDAY, Jessica settled the king in with his first visitor and grabbed her tablet to head upstairs to his closet. It amazed her that she could so easily move around the palace that had formerly been forbidden to her. Depending upon which route she took, she sometimes came across a member of palace security, but after checking her credentials the first time, they now waved her on.

That morning when she flipped through the suits and shirts in Mateo's closet, an odd wistfulness flitted through her. There was a certain intimacy to touching the things he would wear. But that wasn't it. She missed him. Not the guy who dictated letters or offered her the cream for her coffee at breakfast. She missed the person she could really talk to. After their picnic the week before, he'd almost become someone else, but so had she. Their sense of decorum stood strong.

They should be proud.

Should be.

And maybe someday she would be, but right now, she missed what they'd had in their few private encounters. She'd never really been herself like this before. Open. Honest. She'd learned quickly in her marriage that topics or needs that caused arguments usually weren't worth mentioning, until the scales of their relationship had tipped so far in her husband's favor there was no bringing them back.

She hadn't minded. Their life together had been fine. Good usually. But vanilla.

She winced.

After a decade of being divorced, looking at her marriage objectively, she had to admit there had been no passion. No excitement. Just day-to-day taking care of business. At the time, she'd felt lucky that her relationship was so calm. Now, knowing she'd held back to keep him from yelling at her, she recognized she'd sacrificed herself, her wistfulness, her dreams, her passion.

Things were not like that with Mateo. He was strong enough to handle an opinion different than his. He was strong enough to handle *her*. If they ever got the chance to make love, it would be explosive.

The closet door opened, and she just barely held back a gasp as she spun around to see who it was. When she saw Mateo, she clutched her chest. "Your Majesty! Is everything all right?"

He displayed the cuff of a white shirt that was currently coffee colored. "I spilled my drink."

Their gazes met as the door closed behind him. The last time they were alone, they'd spoken honestly about having an affair. After the thoughts she'd been having about him—about them—seeing him brought ripples of arousal.

She swallowed and pointed at a row of shirts in the closet. "You have plenty of shirts you can change into."

"Yes. Thank you."

The appropriate thing to do right at that moment would have been to leave. But her heart rate had ticked upward as a million possibilities raced through her brain. They were alone at certain points every day, but never alone like this. Where the chance that someone could burst in was almost nil.

He slipped out of his jacket and reality stole her breath. She could not be in this room when he removed his shirt. She was about to head for the door, but she stopped her foot when it wanted to move. She'd have to walk by him. Might brush against him.

Meaning, she should take a circuitous route around the center island and bench for putting on shoes. It would walk her so far away there be no risk that they'd accidentally touch.

She headed that way.

"Stop!"

She froze.

"Seriously, you're going to walk twenty feet out of your way just so you don't have to get close to me?"

"It seemed prudent."

He tossed his jacket to a bench. "Oh, the hell with prudent." Quick strides brought him to her. He said, "I miss talking to you," then he kissed her.

The words might have been correct, but the kiss was the truth.

Warm and desperate enough to border on wild, the kiss stole her breath and sent need careening through her. Whatever they had, it was strong and forceful. And unpredictable. And wonderful.

But she wasn't the kind of woman to daydream about someone she couldn't have, and he wasn't the kind to kiss someone he wasn't *allowed* to have.

He broke the kiss and stared into her eyes. "What's the matter with us?"

She laughed. "You mean because we can't keep our hands off each other when we know anything between us would be wrong?"

"It *can't* be wrong. Inappropriate maybe, but something this strong can't be wrong."

"Attractions are wrong all the time."

"This isn't just attraction."

She stepped away, shaking her head. "No. There's something here."

"Something I've never felt before."

She caught his gaze. "Something I've never felt before. And I was sure I was in love at one point."

"Maybe it's just like one of those fluke things that is exciting then runs its course and fizzles?"

She hated to even consider that. "Maybe."

He looked at the ceiling, then back at her. "But even if it is…aren't you curious?"

Waves of relief billowed out on the laugh that escaped her. "Oh, absolutely."

"I mean, even if it's not forever, it's certainly a once-in-a-lifetime thing."

"Yes." She paused and frowned. "Actually, that might be the problem. What we feel hasn't happened before to either one of us, and it won't happen again."

"In a way, that's nice to think about." He blew his breath out on a sigh. "You know…I never even considered something like this existed, but I like it. Which makes it seem like a mistake to ignore it."

"Yes. I feel that too."

They stood there, in his huge dressing room closet, both contemplative. Or maybe both thinking the same thing and afraid to mention it.

She swallowed. "I'm guessing this is why people have affairs."

He groaned. "Don't make it sound sordid. I *like* you."

She cautiously stepped toward him. "I like you too." Pressing her hands against his shirtfront, she said, "Who would have ever thought a king could be so normal."

He snorted. "I was a bad kid, a mischievous teenager…and let's not even talk about my years at university. I've been normal."

"Which is probably why you're so understanding with your kids."

He said, "Probably," but the feeling of her hands on his chest, even through a shirt, were driving him crazy. He wanted to scoop her off the floor and carry her to his bed and make passionate love. But he had people waiting for him.

Anger and the unfairness of the situation made him pull away. "I better go downstairs."

"Yes. Me too."

But their gazes clung.

He squeezed his eyes shut. "You know, we're not going to get rid of these feelings unless we act on them."

She smiled. "Maybe I don't want to get rid of these feelings."

"You're saying you'd spend your life pining for me?" He frowned. "That would be fun?"

"It's better to have loved and lost…"

"In order for that to be true, we'd have to have loved—which means act on this."

She laughed, grabbed her tablet from the big island and headed for the door. "You overthink.

Just enjoy the warm, fuzzy feelings. That's more than a lot of people get."

He watched her walk to the door. The warm, fuzzy feelings did something totally different to his body than they did to hers because he would need a few minutes before he'd be able to go downstairs. He slipped out of the soiled shirt and into another, but as he was buttoning his fingers froze.

What if they *were* overthinking? He was a smart guy. He'd already planned one private picnic. He owned properties. She had an apartment—

He also had a security detail.

A driver.

Children who came looking for him when he least expected—

He groaned. Damn it! He would figure this out.

Because her friendship mattered to him as much as the romance. He liked talking to her, being genuine with someone. He could not believe he was supposed to ignore this.

Maybe that was the point? The romantic part of their relationship might be wrong, but their friendship wasn't. Maybe what his instincts were telling him was that he should be happy for the friendship and not lose it by reaching for something that couldn't be.

At the end of the day, when his meetings were over and guests were gone, he pulled up the schedules of all three of his children. All three had dinner plans.

He walked into Jessica's office. "Ms. Smith?"

Her head snapped up. Her eyes held the sincerity and determination of an assistant focused on seeing to his every official need.

"I was wondering if you played chess."

"Chess?"

"Yes." He motioned for her to join him in his office and walked over to the sofa. He'd set up a board on the table in front of it.

She laughed gaily. "I love chess. I just don't have anyone to play with."

He spread his hands. "Well, here I am. With my kids growing older I find myself without players too."

She inched toward the table, as if confused. He'd moved the chair closer to the chessboard for convenience of play. She slowly made her way to it, as if still not sure what was going on.

He returned to the door between their offices and closed it. "I was thinking about us today and realized we might not be able to have anything romantic, but I didn't want to lose our friendship."

Understanding filled her blue eyes. "I agree."

He removed his suit jacket, hung it on the back of the sofa and sat in front of the chessboard. "I'll be black. Give you the advantage."

"Going first doesn't automatically give me an advantage."

"Recent stats show that white wins fifty-six percent of the time. If that holds true today, the next time we play we'll flip for it."

She laughed. "Okay." She took her seat. "This feels weird."

"The chair is uncomfortable? Or the situation feels weird?"

"The situation. I'm playing chess with a king."

"No. You're playing chess with a guy who likes your company and your friendship. Chess gives us a chance to talk. If anybody walks in, they'll think we're getting to know each other...which is also true."

"Makes sense..." She eased her pawn to a new position. "And is very diplomatic of you, Your Majesty."

He studied the board. She'd made the classic King's Pawn opening.

He countered.

Focused on the board, she said nothing.

Neither said anything for three moves.

But in a way that was good. They really were playing the game. But he liked talking to her more. "Have you been looking at next week's schedule?"

Studying the board for her next move, she said, "Yes. I always try to get a jump on things."

"Good. And you noticed there were still empty afternoons?"

She nodded. "Three. I figured they'd fill up in the last minute."

"Sometimes they do. Sometimes they don't. Keep your eye on those. Try to save at least one so I can schedule some riding time."

She looked over at him. "Okay."

"I always consider the afternoons off, when I can sneak away, as making up for the times I work around the clock."

"During big crises?"

"We might be a quiet, simple country but we still have union walkout threats, border nudges, terrorist threats."

"I've never heard of anything like that."

"That's because we keep it under control. We don't hide things from the press but if a threat doesn't materialize because we neutralized it, there's no reason to tell anyone."

She looked like she might disagree but said, "Okay."

"I've also spent late nights walking the floor hoping Olivia and Joshua choose good mates."

She laughed heartily. "That I understand. I've done that myself."

"Olivia is aware that whoever she marries will live in a spotlight."

Jessica didn't answer for a second as she pondered her next play. She moved her game piece then said, "Do you ever consider arranging a marriage for her?"

He winced and moved his bishop, ending the

game. "My arranged marriage was fine, but empty. I'm not sure I'd want to do that to her."

She gaped at him.

"Are you surprised that I beat you so quickly or confused about me not wanting to arrange a marriage for Olivia?"

"I'm not happy you beat me so quickly. I agree about Olivia."

He reset the board. "Wanna be black?"

She snorted. "I'll stay with the white. And before you get too proud, it's been years since I played. I'll be looking for chess online when I get home so I can practice and be ready for the next session."

During the second game, they shifted easily from discussing Olivia finding a mate to Josh being one of the smartest people Mateo had ever met. "And I've met a lot of people."

She lifted her gaze from the board. "Do you wish he was your successor?"

"Not even a little bit. He's perfect where he is. He's the detail guy. Olivia has heart. She likes the details, the numbers, the logic, but then she considers the human side of things and some of her decisions are interesting."

She smiled at him for a second, then she said, "You know what else is interesting? All this time we've been talking about Josh and Oliva, and their futures and you've never once mentioned Sabrina."

He sucked in a big breath. "I don't eliminate her from conversations deliberately. Josh and Olivia are already on their career paths and talking about them is basically talking about work. But I also think that's part of why it's my fault that Sabrina is an attention seeker. I've inadvertently made her feel like there is no place for her. But there is. If you look at the big picture, Olivia as queen and Josh as head of parliament… Sabrina could be our 'presence' outside the country."

"Like an ambassador?"

"A royal visiting a country is more than an ambassador. There's a power to the position of being part of a royal family. Plus, if you consider her personality, she has the qualities of someone who has a heart like her older sister and a brain like her brother…with the personality that wins people over."

"From what I've seen of her, yes, she would be very good at that. Have you told her yet?"

He took a breath. "I'm facing some delicate timing. If I tell her too soon, she could get cocky and arrogant."

"Your other two kids knew their positions when they were in grammar school, and they did just fine."

He inclined his head. "Yes. They did. But Sabrina is different from her brother and sister. I'm not sure how I missed teaching her this, but she hasn't yet learned that we serve the people of our country. She still sees people as serving her."

"I know how you missed it. You didn't have to teach Olivia and Josh that they served the kingdom because they knew they had a position they were stepping into and they knew service was part of it. Without looking at a future in the government, Sabrina didn't have that sensibility."

"Huh. I never thought of that." He smiled. "That's how I missed teaching her that."

Jessica shrugged. "I think so." She peeked over at him. "So, what you need to do now is watch for opportunities to tell her there's a place for her. Once she sees herself having a position, you'll be able to help her shift the way she looks at things. Especially, the idea that she serves her people."

During game three, they talked some more about their country, his job and the cottage she hoped to someday buy. He even teased that she could find land on the outer edge of the royal estate and build her cottage there.

"Didn't you say that was a natural park or something?"

"It's a forest. People use it like a national park, but really, it's nothing because we keep it that way."

"So, you'd have to sell me the land?"

"No. We don't own it…we just keep track of it."

She laughed, but her laugh turned into a yawn. "Oh, my goodness. I'm so sorry."

He rose. "No. You're tired." Glancing at his

watch, he said, "I shouldn't have kept you so long."
He walked to his desk and pressed a button on his
phone. "Philip, have someone bring Ms. Smith's
car to the front entry. We worked a little late tonight."

With the office staff gone, the motor pool wasn't
surprised to hear from him directly. Philip said,
"Yes, Your Majesty."

He faced her again. "Can I see you out?"

"No. I'm fine. I appreciate not having to walk
across the parking lot though."

He sniffed. "Arthur snagged that perk years
ago. When he arrives, he actually pulls his car
up to the front entrance and has one of the guards
park it, then he has the car brought back to him
when he leaves."

"I would really like that."

"Consider it done."

She walked to the door separating their offices
and he followed her. "Tonight was fun. The next
time, I promise I won't bore you with talk about
my kids."

She laughed. "I could tell you about my cro-
cheting... Oh, or the book I'm reading."

She gave the title, and he nodded. "I'll read it
too."

"We'll be a book club!"

He stepped closer and gave in to the irresistible urge to run his hand along her back. "A private book club."

She smiled at him. "Yes."

His other hand went to her waist of its own volition. He didn't see a battle taking place in her eyes. She was too busy smiling, drifting closer to him.

He swore he could feel the chemistry he'd been fighting all evening rising like mist over a lake. Subtle, but so natural there was no stopping it.

Knowing this part of the palace was empty, he gave in to his instinct to kiss her, even though this was only supposed to be a friendship evening together. His hands on her waist itched to drift lower, but she broke their kiss.

"My car's waiting for me."

He bent to kiss her again. "No. It'll take a minute for Philip to send someone to take that walk you now won't have to make and get your car."

She laughed but kissed him back. What started simple and easy ramped up and became a passionate exchange. Their tongues twined. His hands roved. Her hands slid from his shoulders down his back, igniting little fires everywhere they went.

The thought that they couldn't go any further sent fury screaming through him. Nothing had ever seemed so natural or so right. Yet it wasn't to be.

He attempted to break the kiss, but impulse had taken over and kept coming up with new ideas for how to kiss her, where to touch her. He'd made love before, many times, but he'd never felt the guttural instinct that rolled through him, almost demanding that he take what he wanted.

The intercom on his phone buzzed. "Your Majesty?"

He stopped; confusion froze him for a few seconds, then he raced to the other side of the desk and pressed the button. "Yes, Philip?"

"The car is here. I'm about to clock out. Dale is replacing me."

He sucked in some air and looked over at Jessica, who was running her fingers through her hair, straightening it. Because he'd messed it up. And he wanted to do it again…and more.

The injustice of it spiraled through him, but he said, "She is on her way now."

"Thank you, Your Majesty."

"Good night, Philip. We'll see you tomorrow."

He disconnected the call and glanced at Jessica. Their eyes met. He could see the same regret in hers that he knew filled his. She wasn't upset that he'd kissed her. She was as upset as he was that they'd had to stop, and she had to leave.

It tore him apart to watch her walk out the door.

CHAPTER EIGHT

THE FOLLOWING MORNING, Jessica stepped out of the shower and looked at herself in her full-length mirror. She'd always been average sized, but exercise kept her tummy from being overly squishy, her butt tight and her breasts from sagging. She wouldn't mind if Mateo saw her naked.

She took a quick breath, pushed that thought out of her brain and strode out of her bathroom to get herself dressed for the day.

Her work clothes were laid out on the bed, but when she picked up her bra, she grimaced. She'd always considered herself young at heart. Yet here she was about to put on a sensible bra and granny panties.

She carried them back to her dresser and rummaged for the pink bra and panties she'd bought on her last internet shopping trip. She couldn't remember why she'd bought them—they were probably on sale—but she was glad she had. Just as her cottage in the woods was beginning to feel like she was giving up on life, her old lady underwear made her feel frumpy, so it would now be replaced. All of it. In fact, she might just burn it because it reminded her of a time in her life where she'd clung to anything sensible that she could find, desperate for normalcy. But things were changing. *She* was changing. She would follow the impulses wherever they led.

Happy with that plan, she slid a light blue sweater and black skirt over her pink undies and all but bounced into her kitchen. She wouldn't let her brain tiptoe toward the idea that her feelings for Mateo were giving her a youthful glow and causing her to focus on how she was still young, still vital—

And could be happy.

Her hand paused over the coffeemaker. For heaven's sake. That's what this weird feeling was. Happiness. The kind of joy she believed she'd never find again. What they had might not go anywhere permanently, but even the flirting and kissing were changing her, reminding her that there was a lot of life left to be *lived*. Not just endured.

Even if she never had a full-blown romance with Mateo, he'd pulled her out of that funk. She could at least admit that.

When she reached the palace guard station, Franco greeted her. "I hear you have new parking accommodations."

"You know Arthur's out for two months, right?"

"Gallbladder surgery."

"Well, I'm his replacement."

He laughed. "Yeah, Arthur finagled parking privileges a few years ago."

She smiled at Franco. "Now, they're a thing."

And just like that she was over her fear of people knowing she worked for the king and her distaste for getting privilege. She knew she'd held back on a lot of things because she didn't like being seen or being recognized. But inside the gates of this palace no one was looking at her as Eleanore Smith's mom. Here, she was the king's personal assistant.

When she entered her office, Mateo was already there. "Ms. Smith. You're early."

She shrugged out of her coat, ready to dive into work. "Is there anything I can help you with? Find for you?"

He told her about an old treaty with a country that no longer existed. "I need to refresh my memory about the terms of the agreement."

"Really? With a country that hasn't existed for ten years?"

He laughed as she sat at her desk and started typing on her computer keyboard. She'd quickly learned that the old physical filing system was antiquated, and it would take a compass and sherpa to help her find anything in that mess. But it didn't matter because everything existed somewhere digitally. Those files were sleek and elegant and more easily navigated.

"The land still exists. The boundaries are the same. The government is just different. And let's just say they're a little full of themselves. I want to remind their president of the terms his predecessor agreed to and hope he realizes I won't be bullied. But first I need to show it to my cabinet, see if they still agree with what we'd penned ten years ago."

"Ah. Found it." She twisted around to face him. "Do you want it printed?"

"Email it to me." He smiled. "Ready for breakfast?"

She rose from her desk. "Yes. I'm starving. I didn't eat dinner last night."

He winced. "Sorry about that."

She nearly stretched up to kiss him but caught herself just in time. When they were working, those impulses were out of place. And she would control them.

She laughed. "It was worth it. But now I'm super hungry for whatever the chef has in mind."

He motioned for her to precede him to the door. He didn't make any references to her saying it was worth it. His eyes didn't even ask if she'd actually been talking about their make-out session being worth missing a meal or the chess games. With the exception of her near-miss with wanting to stretch up and kiss him, in this minute they were nothing but a boss and his personal assistant.

And it didn't feel odd. This felt as right as kissing him had the night before. It wasn't as if she were two people but more like they had a professional relationship and a personal one and they were growing accustomed to separating those roles.

They walked up the stairs together and down the hallway to a side entrance to the royal king's quarters, the one she'd been instructed to use when she needed to go into his closet.

He pointed to the left to a hall she'd never walked down. "There's a really fancy foyer at the end of that corridor. In case you're ever asked to escort someone up here to see me, that's the entry you would use. The elevator will take you right to it."

"Do you think I should get a tour of this place, so I'll always know where to go?"

He frowned. "We've used up two and a half weeks of Arthur's leave of absence. If he doesn't retire, you probably don't need an official tour."

She heard the bit of sadness in his voice and felt a corresponding sadness in the pit of her stomach. Working for him had been so much fun and so good for her that she hated to see it end—

But that wasn't the reason her chest tightened. She'd never had feelings like these for another person. Never felt so connected. Never felt so sexy and beautiful. Never longed to make love with someone the way she did him.

It didn't matter. That was a consideration for

another day. Right now, she was a personal assistant about to have breakfast and go over her king's schedule.

They eased into the dining room to find Sabrina and Olivia already there.

Olivia stood. "Good morning, Your Majesty."

He pulled out Jessica's chair for her. She hesitated. He'd never done that before. Still, this was the first time they had entered together.

He sighed. "Olivia, right now, I'm your dad. Not your king."

Olivia took her seat again. "I know, but some days it's fun to go overboard with the pomp and circumstance."

He shook his head as he sat at the head of the table. "And good morning to you, too, Sabrina."

She mumbled, "Morning, Dad," into her oatmeal.

"You're eating oatmeal?"

"I'm not really hungry and I thought this was the most inconsequential thing to waste."

Mateo laughed. Olivia rolled her eyes. Jessica didn't react at all. She was at the table only as an employee.

Nevil came in and took the king's breakfast order, then Jessica's. As soon as he was gone, Olivia said, "I'm actually here because I want to hear your schedule. If you have nothing going on tonight, my oversight committee is meeting. It's been about six months since you attended one of our meetings and I just thought it was time for you to sit in. You know…let us see we're not forgotten."

"No one is ever forgotten."

"I know that, and you know that," Olivia said. "But an appearance from you always reignites a committee's fire."

He shrugged. "Sure. What time's the meeting?"

"Seven. We typically work about three hours."

"Okay."

"Thanks."

A few minutes later, Nevil returned with their breakfast. Jessica dug into her eggs and bacon like the starving woman that she was. When she reached for her coffee, she noticed Sabrina staring at her, studying her.

With the youngest royal child at the table, the mood of the meal was considerably more casual. She couldn't believe Sabrina disliked the relaxed atmosphere, but she might dislike an outsider eating with them.

The easiest way to make herself look like she had a purpose at this table was to bring out the schedule. Olivia had asked about it and received an answer without actually having to go over the day's events. But her purpose at breakfast with this family was to go over the schedule.

She lifted the tablet from the chair beside her and tapped the screen. "So? Ready to hear the day's schedule?"

Mateo pointed at her half-eaten meal. "Finish. We have plenty of time."

"No. I'm fine."

She began with that morning's meetings and while Olivia perked up, Sabrina sighed and pulled her spoon through the oatmeal she wasn't eating. Occasionally, Olivia would begin a short discussion of a meeting or a visitor, and Jessica would use that time to eat more of her food.

It was a very smooth operation. They went over the schedule. Everyone ate in between line items and the meal was both delicious and productive.

With the schedule read, Olivia left.

Sabrina sighed.

Jessica wanted to ask if she was okay, but that wasn't her place. Besides, Mateo had said if she noticed one of the kids behaving strangely, she should be discreet.

Plus, looking at Sabrina's red eyes, she wondered if she had a hangover…or if she'd come in late and gotten up too early.

Mateo glanced at her. "I know we don't go over my weekend schedule until Friday, but could you check to see if I have an event for Eliminate Hunger?"

She picked up her tablet again. Eliminate Hunger was a European charity and she'd seen it on the schedule on Saturday. Still, she double-checked.

"Yes. On Saturday."

"Is it in their facility—the warehouse?"

"Yes." She hit the line item to access the details. "You are to go to their warehouse for a tour, then present a check as a gift from Pocetak."

He sat back. "The last time I went, I wore a suit and felt like a stuffy old man. Can you put together something like a cashmere sweater and… not jeans."

"How about kakis?"

"Yes. Or something like gray trousers. Maybe put two or three options together for me. I don't want to look like a stodgy old man. I want to look like a king who is involved—aware of things. Not just a guy who comes in once a year and pretends."

"Okay."

As she made notes on her tablet, Mateo turned to Sabrina. "I'd love for you to come with me to that event."

She gaped at him. "It's on a Saturday!"

"I know, but I've been thinking about your place in the kingdom, and I have to admit that I've always seen you as our ambassador."

Her face scrunched with distaste. "You want me to be an ambassador?"

"No. I want you to be *the* ambassador. Not for one country, but our point of contact with all charities and humanitarian efforts. You'd be the face of the family's philanthropy."

Sabrina still gaped at him. "You and Olivia and Joshua already do those things."

"We fold it into our schedules. But with you

spearheading that part of our rule, you could turn it into a cohesive effort."

For a few seconds, Sabrina said nothing. She glanced from her father to Jessica. Then she looked at her uneaten oatmeal.

"Sabrina," Mateo said, bringing her attention to him again. "This could be the best job in the palace. You could do so much good, but you could also bring hope. I'm telling you now before you go to university, so you can think it through and consider the kinds of classes that would assist you."

"Okay."

Mateo laughed. "I thought you would be happier."

She took a breath and peered at Jessica again, before turning her attention to her oatmeal. "I'm just a little tired still. Late night last night."

Jessica wished she could fade into the wallpaper or disappear at will. The second glance from Sabrina had been extremely uncomfortable. Even if the late night and lack of sleep explained her sour mood, Mateo's youngest did not like Jessica at the table.

Knowing this was the perfect time to make an easy exit, she rose.

"I will see you in the office, Your Majesty."

Mateo rose. "Thank you, Ms. Smith."

As she walked out of the dining room, she heard Mateo say, "So you will go with me on Saturday?"

She didn't stick around to hear Sabrina's reply.

If Mateo needed help or advice, he would ask. But she had the feeling that once she left, Sabrina would be honest with her dad, and they would work this out.

Because, truth be told, if someone offered her the chance to be a goodwill ambassador, handing out checks, giving hope…she would call it her dream job and she was fairly certain Sabrina would see that too.

She continued walking down the stairway and would have considered the breakfast a successful first step to Mateo getting Sabrina on the road to her place in the monarchy—

Except for the looks Sabrina had given her, the way she'd studied her, as if she were looking for something.

Or trying to figure something out.

Oh, Lord. What if she'd searched her on the internet and found Ellie's high-profile troubles? What if she'd figured out Jessica had begun using her middle name to throw people off track?

No. Even if she figured that out, there were so many Smiths in every corner of the internet that it would take a while to make the connection.

At the bottom of the steps, she took a long breath and reminded herself that Sabrina was tired, and the king's youngest daughter could simply be curious about the person who'd replaced Arthur.

At eighteen, she was still a kid. Her concern

would be about her dad's staff—not who Jessica was personally, only who she was in terms of her position in the palace.

Actually, it made more sense to think Sabrina was trying to figure out how to deal with her dad's temporary assistant, if she could trick Jessica, fool her if she needed a favor.

That she would watch out for.

CHAPTER NINE

WHEN THE KING was in his third meeting of the afternoon, Jessica slipped out of the office and up to his closet. She entered his quarters through a side door that opened on the same foyer they'd used that morning to get to the dining room.

Instead of racing to get to his closet door as she usually did, she paused and looked down the corridors to the right and left.

She knew the back way to the dining room, but now she also knew that the family quarters had a main entrance. It was also obvious this side entrance was a private entrance for Mateo's quarters that also led to the main living space. She wondered if there were side entrances like this one for his kids' living spaces. If there were, that would make personal quarters something like apartments. Meaning, people could come and go as they pleased.

Though the family lived together, they could stay in their own quarters if they wanted privacy or alone time.

She walked down the silent corridor to the door that led to the closet. The fact that she could enter the king's closet without going into his quarters also did not surprise her. She supposed he had a front door of a sort that probably opened onto a sitting room. He might even have a small kitchen. But with this side door, his assistant didn't have to traipse through his private space to get to the place she needed to go to put together outfits for him when he needed her help.

She didn't mind being kept out of his private space, but curiosity about the way he lived filled her as she stepped into his dressing room/closet. Especially when she saw that the door to his bathroom had been left open.

She tiptoed over and sighed when she saw the elegant room. A huge walk-in shower. A stand-alone claw-foot tub with a tray for tea or books or even reading a document if that was what he wanted to do while relaxing in the huge tub.

Shiny white tile covered the floor, and four mirrors were strategically placed. Two above the sinks of the bleached wood double vanity and two full-length mirrors.

The main light was a chandelier, but each mirror had lights above it. Pale blue towels were rolled into cylinders and stored in an open shelf for easy access.

She walked inside and twirled around. It was huge, bright, clean and probably had every convenience known to mankind tucked away in the drawers and shelves. But more than anything else, it was peaceful, tranquil…like a spa.

She stopped twirling when she noticed the door on the other end of the bathroom. This one wasn't open, but one little flick of a doorknob would fix that.

Temptation rose. Nine chances out of ten his bedroom was just beyond that door. Even more curiosity flitted through her. It would be so easy to open the door and take a quick peek—

No. That wasn't right. Technically, his private space wasn't her business. She would behave.

She turned to leave but pivoted to face the door again. No. This was not the time for behaving. She might never get this chance again. She just wanted to see his room. It was no big deal. Normal curiosity.

Though she was alone, she tiptoed to the door and opened it only a crack to look inside.

"Find anything you like, Ms. Smith?"

Her heart about exploded out of her chest. She spun around. "You scared me!"

He chuckled. "I probably should have done something, so you'd hear me, but it was just funny catching you." He sighed. "I know you're curious. *Everybody* is." He motioned to the opened door. "Go ahead. I have nothing to hide."

Guilt stopped her from moving. "I'm sorry. I above everybody else should respect your privacy.

I know what it's like to have everybody wonder about everything in your life."

"I don't look at it that way. I think everybody's curious about how *everybody* else lives. Not just royals or people in the news. Have you ever used somebody's bathroom and opened their medicine cabinet?"

She pressed her hand to her chest. "No!"

"Sixty percent of people do."

"Sixty percent, really? Did you take a poll?"

He laughed. "I get a lot of information sent to me. Some of it is valuable… Some of it's about nosy visitors and weird statistics." He motioned to the door again. "But it's natural to be curious. Besides, I'm glad you're up here. We can choose my sweater for Saturday."

It finally hit her that he was supposed to be in a meeting. And even if he wasn't, he didn't go to his quarters willy-nilly. "What are you doing up here?"

"Meeting ended early. I'm a firm believer in stopping things when I've gotten my way… No sense continuing to talk and giving people a chance to change their minds."

She snickered. "I get that."

"Besides, I was hoping to find you up here. You know…to take a look at those sweaters…and maybe entice you into another make-out session."

The easy way he said it sent warmth fluttering through her, stopping in her heart that sort of melted with happiness. She loved that he liked her.

She stepped over and flattened her hands on his chest. "So all that stuff about medicine cabinets was a lie?"

He caught her fingers, then brought them to his lips to kiss. "Nope. That's true. But when I got up here and saw you so close to the privacy of my bedroom, I realized we'd never get another chance like this. Right now, everybody in my office suite assumes I'm in a meeting. And your job requires that you move around. No one looks for you."

"Unless they're trying to find you."

"No one is looking for me."

"That's true." She stood on tiptoes and kissed him. He shifted his hands to her back, letting them roam as he brought her closer and kissed her deeply. Everything inside her blossomed to life. It seemed impossible that they weren't meant to be together. Then she remembered that not being able to have something permanent didn't mean they couldn't have anything at all.

And he was right. They might never have a chance like this again.

When he broke the kiss, she took his hand and guided him into the bedroom. With the drapes drawn, the room was dark. She stopped at the foot of his bed, then laughed. "Really? A black comforter?"

"I didn't like the flowery stuff housecleaning kept putting on the bed. So I asked for black."

"You are such a guy." She stepped close, sliding her hands up his shirtfront until they eased under his jacket, and she could nudge it off.

Seeing her intention, he let his suit coat fall far enough that he could remove it. "I am a guy." And right now, he was feeling that more than he had in decades. The sensation of her hands on him coupled with the knowledge that she was seducing him, nearly rendered him speechless.

She paused and caught his gaze. "Your Majesty, I think I should tell you I wore my matching pink bra and panties."

Desire ratcheted through him, but so did a horrible fear. Was all this too easy? Too wonderful? Was he being played? "You planned this?"

"No. But I want it. I think I knew that this morning when I got dressed."

He studied her eyes. As much as he yearned to make love with her, he had to remind her of the truth. "This won't go anywhere—can't go anywhere."

She began unbuttoning his shirt. "Doesn't matter. I think you and I are meant for the moment." She met his gaze. "You know. We're meant to enjoy what we have while we have it. We can't plan for tomorrow, and we can't take this out in public," she said, motioning around his bedroom.

"But maybe that's what makes what we have so special. It's ours. No one else's."

The idea of having something private, special, was breathlessly tempting to a man who'd shared his entire life with the world. He'd never had anything that was just his. And now, here she was. Just his. Not something to be shared or analyzed. Simply enjoyed.

He lifted her chin with his index finger to kiss her deeply and was rewarded with her sigh of pleasure. Then his hands slid down to the bottom of her sweater and began to ease it upward.

"Let's see what the pink bra looks like."

She laughed. "You know if you tease me too long, I could return that favor."

He pulled the sweater over her head, examined the pretty pink lace garment. "I like it."

She kissed him. "Sweet talker, but as I said, turnabout is fair play."

"I'm not worried. We only have a half an hour before we're missed. One of us is going to have to go downstairs before the other to throw everybody off our trail, cutting another five minutes off. I can tease and you can't retaliate."

She laughed, and he kissed her, pulling her close to enjoy the feel of her. But he still wore his shirt. With a quick curse, he pulled back and rid himself of the unwanted garment. Just as quickly, he found the zipper on her skirt and got rid of that too.

While he worked on that, she undid all the connections for his trousers, and they fell to the floor. Not about to argue with efficiency, he stepped out of them.

"Twenty minutes, you say?" She gave him a swift nudge that caused him to fall on the bed. "We don't have any time to waste."

He caught her hand and yanked her to the bed with him. She fell willingly into his arms. Nothing had ever felt like this. Free. Spontaneous. So oddly different than his role as a royal, a king, that the sensation of being himself, only himself, flooded him with ridiculous need for her. For everything about her. Her laugh. Her sighs. The way she talked. The way she felt so right. The way she hadn't been afraid to kiss him. From the very beginning there'd been something wonderful between them.

The smoothness of her skin shot a burst of fire through him. He told himself to go slow, to remember everything, but when his lips met her smooth flesh, the temptation to quickly taste every inch of her was too much to ignore. Her soft sighs let him know she enjoyed it as much as he did and something inside him exploded with the need to give her pleasure.

But when he brought them face-to-face again, aligning their bodies so he could absorb the feeling of her skin against his, she turned the tables. Running her tongue from his neck to his navel, she teased and tempted him until he rolled her over and reversed their roles.

He loved the spontaneity of it, the way need dictated action. He rained kisses from her neck to her breasts, stopping to savor their taste while she ran her hands down his back.

But their game became very serious as arousal and instincts he didn't even know he had roared through him igniting his blood. He joined them in a rush of adrenaline-fueled hunger that took over and wouldn't stop until he was inside her.

Then the unexpected happened. They both stopped.

She took a long, pleasure-filled breath.

He simply lost himself in the moment. He didn't know if they'd ever be able to do this again. Savoring the feeling of her warmth wrapped around him and the wonder of their connection, was part of his need. The thing he'd remember forever, if only because it was a wonderful, but passing gift.

They began to move, slower this time, at a pace laden with enjoyment and awe. He didn't want to think she'd ever felt this arousal-filled bliss with another man because he'd certainly never felt it with another woman. He shoved the jealousy out of his mind and gave as much as he took.

When they reached the peak, intense pleasure exploded in every cell of his body. Her cry of delight told him she felt the same.

After a few seconds absorbing the unexpected

wonder of it all, they broke apart and he rolled her to his side of the bed with him, their heads on the same pillow.

"I don't know where I'd protest, but if we don't get the chance to do that again, I will find someone to complain to."

She laughed. "It was pretty amazing."

He shifted to his side so he could look at her face. "*You* are amazing. You make me feel so different. It's as if I spent my whole life as a role… heir to the throne, then king…and everything sort of bowed to that. With you, I'm just me."

She smiled and twined their bare legs. "With you, I'm just me too."

Need for her spiraled through him again. He would have cursed it because their time was melting away, but it was all so new, so intense, so wonderful, he let himself enjoy it. "Why did we have to get to fifty before we found this?"

She shrugged. "Maybe we had some life to live before we could appreciate it."

He took her hand and kissed her fingers. He loved the philosopher in her—the smart person who could counsel him with his kids and keep him grounded—as much as he loved her smooth skin, her delicate hands, the sheer femininity that seemed to reach out and pull him to her.

"Maybe." He ran his hand along her thigh and her belly. Savoring again. Not just the reality of being with her, but the mood, the moment.

"We're going to have to figure out a way to find some more time together before Arthur comes back."

And just like that she broke the mood and brought sadness to his joy when she gave them a timetable.

The unfairness of it shot through him, but he understood what she was saying. There were too many hurdles to maneuver around for them to even daydream about having this relationship forever.

They had to make the best of the here and now.

CHAPTER TEN

THEY DRESSED QUICKLY with Mateo leaving first by way of a back balcony so that when he entered his office, he could make it appear he'd been in the garden thinking. She redressed then shuffled through his closet looking for three sweaters, shirts and trousers to lay out on the table. If anybody missed her, she could talk about searching for clothing for the king's Saturday outing.

Walking out of the closet into the hall, then the foyer, then the staircase, the joy of making love with him almost overwhelmed her. She loved touching him and having him touch her, but there was more. Making love intensified the heart connection she'd always felt with him. The sense that they belonged together. She knew that would grow every time they were together like that. Still, his schedule was so busy, and everybody wanted to know where he was every minute of the day, that she honestly despaired that they'd ever get to do it again—

But maybe that was a good thing. In spite of

her suggestion that they try to find more times to be alone, the thought of someone catching them and potentially thrusting her into the news cycle again tightened her chest. She remembered not being able to pull into her own driveway because it was filled with people from the press. She remembered staying in a hotel with her daughter to avoid them then waking to find the lobby teeming with people who peppered them with questions.

Being with Mateo might be delicious but a real relationship with him came at a price. And not just for her. His sedate, quiet palace would explode with speculation. From reporters, yes. But he also had kids and a dedicated staff—

How would they see this?

Would she be a gold digger and he be a foolish man falling for a woman whose daughter might have also seduced a man in power?

That's how the press had painted Eleanore, a gold digger looking to blackmail the politician and when he wouldn't pay, she trumped up the rape. Would they paint Jessica with the same brush? Would Eleanore's life be torn apart again?

Mateo entered his office trying not to grin. But something about the atmosphere of his workspace brought his mood in line almost automatically, as if his brain instantly made the separation of his private life and his work.

Which was good.

The last thing either he or Jessica wanted was for their behavior to cause people to question things. They needed to conduct themselves as they normally would so no one suspected or guessed they'd become lovers.

The reality of someone finding out they were lovers came tumbling down on him like an avalanche of cold snow. The press would want details. Her identity would come out. Her life would become fodder for speculation. Her daughter's life would be shoved into the limelight again.

He squeezed his eyes shut and sat back in his chair.

And all of that would impact his life, his kids, his *rule*.

This had to stay private. Or maybe stop. Because the ramifications of it becoming public were too horrible to contemplate. If he only had himself to worry about, he might risk it. But throwing Jessica into the public eye again? Or her daughter who'd worked so hard to have a normal life? No. He would not do that to either one of them.

She returned to her office, and he glanced up from his desk, into her room. Their gazes caught. He could see from the seriousness in hers that she'd come to the same conclusions he had. Making love might have been the most wonderful experience of his life, but none of their problems had gone away. None of their reservations had even shrunk. There was no future for them.

They didn't play chess that night. Because he would be going to Olivia's committee meeting, he sent Jessica home at a normal hour. With the motor pool employees seeing her arrivals and her departures, he enjoyed a minute of relief. They were a built-in alibi that Jessica came and went like a normal employee.

His constant stream of visitors also saw nothing but a ruler and his personal assistant. Their breakfast on Thursday was a working breakfast with Olivia and Josh joining them, but Sabrina strolled in on Friday morning.

Jessica went over that day's schedule. Mateo added tidbits. Joshua reminded him of a few points to raise in meetings with certain officials. Olivia simply listened intently. He told them about Sabrina going with him to the Eliminate Hunger event and her potential new position.

Everything had gone back to normal. So normal, his heart sank. His day bored him. His life bored him.

He missed Jessica so much that his focus wobbled.

He considered inviting her up to his closet to choose clothes for the next day—but they'd already done that. He had no reason to ask her to meet him. And he didn't want to make up one.

He said goodbye to her at five, letting her go at a normal quitting time so she could have a nice evening. But his night dragged on and on. His kids had plans, so he told the chef he'd make a sandwich, then sent her and the evening butler home early too.

Then he rattled around in his too-empty palace. If Jessica really did live in a cottage that bordered royal property, he could ride a horse there and no one would be any the wiser.

He frowned. He didn't really need a horse to make that work. He usually didn't give his security detail the slip, but there was a car at his disposal. It was a little something his parents had instituted. They called it their getaway car. They rarely used it. But they'd said that without the availability of that vehicle, they would be prisoners.

He finally understood.

Right now, he felt like a prisoner. There was somewhere he wanted to go. It might not be innocent, but it wasn't illegal. And it was necessary for his sanity.

He changed into jeans and a sweatshirt and took the back way to the garage. Using an old key, he unlocked a side door. He didn't flick on the light. Too much chance someone would see him. He ran his hand along the front fender of the old car, laughing softly as he found his way to the door and hopped inside. After he started the engine, he pulled the hat down his forehead so no one would suspect it was him driving the old relic.

The garage door rattled as it opened, but all

three of the on-duty drivers were out with his kids. Even if there was someone in the motor pool, the huge building would absorb the sound.

He was literally sneaking out and no one knew.

The joy of it nearly overwhelmed him. He took the road behind the garage to a back gate. He stopped at the keypad and input the password and just like that he was on the road, by himself.

He found a parking space in front of Jessica's building, pulled the knit cap even farther down his forehead and walked inside. The four flights of stairs didn't bother him. Freedom rushed through his veins like a drug.

He knocked on her door and when she opened it, he hauled her to him and kissed her.

Jessica was so dazzled, she didn't even consider that they were standing in a public hall, kissing.

When he finally pulled back, he quietly said, "I missed you."

She laughed, but reality suddenly flooded her, and she yanked him into her apartment, quietly closing the door behind him.

"What are you doing!"

"I had to see you." He took off the knit cap and ran his fingers through his hair. "Don't worry. No one knows I left. The kids are all out for the evening. And I ditched my detail by taking my dad's old mental health car."

"Mental health car?"

"I never understood it until tonight. It wasn't that the pressure of the job made him feel he needed a car at his disposal that no one knew about. He just liked getting away sometimes."

"You needed to get away?"

He shrugged out of his hoodie and tossed it to a chair. "I think I got a taste of what normal feels like, and my life suddenly seems like an old camel-hair coat. Restrictive and itchy."

He sat on the sofa.

She sat on the chair. "I'm sorry."

He snorted a laugh. "Why? For making me happy?"

She winced. "Yeah. People don't usually complain about that."

He ran his hands down his face. "I will figure out how to handle this."

She rose and slipped over to the sofa to sit beside him. "Maybe we can figure it out together." She nestled against him and laid her head on his shoulder. "Because since I met you, the life I was planning suddenly seems empty. And I don't want it anymore."

"We are a pair."

"I think we're a matched set. Unfortunately, we don't live in the same china cabinet."

"And we can't."

"No. We can't."

"So how do we handle this?"

"Well, I like that you're here now."

He chuckled. "I like that I'm here too."

"We could spend the time commiserating about how unjust our situation is or we could...you know...make the best of the time."

"Why, Ms. Smith. Are you going to seduce me again?"

She gasped and pushed away so she could look at him. "Again?"

"Well, you did sort of take the lead on Monday. First, you led me into the bedroom." He paused and pretended to ponder. "Then if I remember correctly, you shoved me onto the bed."

"You weren't exactly fighting."

He sobered. "No. I wasn't." He leaned in and kissed her quickly. "But I didn't just come here for sex. I really missed you."

"We saw each other every day this week."

"We worked together every day." He sighed. "I like talking to you. I like being with you."

"I'll tell you what." Too happy to let reality ruin their evening, she rose and took his hand, nudging him to stand too. "We can do all the pillow-talk you want."

"So, you are seducing me."

She sighed. "Oh, you royals. You want everything spelled out."

He laughed, following her into her bedroom.

At the foot of her bed in her extremely frilly bedroom, she slid her hands under his T-shirt and sighed with contentment when she touched his warm skin. Trim and toned his body quivered under even her slightest touch. Answering need whispered inside her, making her bold enough to ease his T-shirt over his head and toss it behind her.

He laughed, caught her by the waist and kissed her greedily. She savored the sensations of his mouth on hers, their tongues mating, their bodies brushing. Then he stepped back a bit to remove her sweater. Even as they kissed, they removed each other's clothes in a frenzy of need that filled her with as much joy as the idea that he'd sneaked away to see her.

She shoved her comforter aside so they could lie on the one indulgence she allowed herself, silk sheets. He sighed as he pulled her to him.

"Interesting expense for a woman saving for retirement."

She laughed. "It's the little things."

He laughed, rolled her to her back and kissed her until neither one of them cared about bedclothes. All she knew at that moment was that he was warm and naked, wrapped around her like someone who couldn't get enough of the feel of her.

They made love slowly, as if being in her apartment—away from the demands of his life—was the real luxury. Inhaling the scent of him as he kissed her neck, she realized it was. She'd never felt the physical longing she did with him, and she ran her leg along his to appreciate it. Making love with her husband had been a sort of paint-by-numbers game. With Mateo the yearning to kiss him and touch him and feel him inside her was so intense her breath fluttered away on a sigh of need. As he kissed his way down her belly, she couldn't stop her hands from coasting along his shoulder muscles, feeling them tremble from her touch.

He kissed his way to her neck again. Warmth and need expanded in her middle and she inched to the right, trying to reposition their bodies to where she wanted them. He read the movement correctly and shifted to enter her, filling her, satisfying one kind of need only to create another.

Every inch of her body prickled with arousal, and she moved with him, intensifying the sensations inside her. Greedy for the feel of him, she let her hands roam as his body did amazing things to her.

When the world exploded with a white-hot light, both groaned with pleasure. She couldn't seem to move. Neither could he.

Eventually he rolled over to the pillow beside hers. Silence surrounded them. She knew why. Every time they made love, they knew it could be the last.

She refused to give voice to that and instead eased over to nestle against him. "You're really kind of wonderful...you know that?"

Sliding his hand down her upper arm, he laughed. "I was just going to tell you the same thing."

She swallowed back the almost automatic reply that it was too bad they didn't belong together, but she refused to allow that into their conversation tonight.

"I've been rethinking the whole cabin in the woods."

He slid up to lean against the headboard. "So you said."

"Yeah, I'm thinking it's out."

"Where would you go?"

"Maybe a city."

"A city? That's like the opposite of what you had planned."

"After meeting you, working with you, I want to be part of things again. You said my cabin plan sounded like I wanted to hide from the world. And maybe I did. But now I don't. I feel like I'm coming back to my normal, energetic self."

"There's no need to move. You are very much a part of things at the palace."

She said, "I try to be," even as she realized their affair might change that. It was another thing she had to think about. Could she stay working for him, feeling things for him, but never seeing him. Never touching him. Never knowing that he felt the same longing for her—

Deciding this wasn't the time for that either, she shifted the conversation to Sabrina.

Nestled together, they talked a bit about his daughter and that slid into discussing the unexpected joy of parenting. Then the unexpected disappointment of a frustrating spouse, and finally, the peace of being single again.

"Not that it doesn't have its problems," Mateo said, stroking her hair. "I mean, I am dateless most of the time."

She laughed. "You became an eligible bachelor. I somehow became a burden on society."

He chuckled at the same time that his stomach rumbled.

She sat up. "Didn't you eat?"

"I had the chef make me a sandwich."

She rolled to get out of bed. "Good as her sandwiches are, it appears it wasn't enough."

He sat up. "Where are you going?"

"I have some homemade vegetable soup. I'm not even going to try to compete with your chef. But I bought a loaf of crusty bread that pairs very well with homemade soup."

He laughed. They both found their clothes and kissed happily as they redressed. Finished first, she raced into the kitchen and by the time he got there the bread was cut and the soup was warming. She served it on her little two-person table by a bay window with a breakfast nook. But before he sat down, she closed the blinds.

"Too bad," he said, taking his seat. "I'll bet your street is fun to watch at night."

"Coffee shop on that side," she said, pointing across the street. "And tavern down that way." She angled her thumb behind her. "Both places attract unique customers." She shrugged. "Sometimes I watch."

The simple sentence tugged at his heart. She was as lonely as he was. They might both have busy lives, but in spite of their children, they were alone.

He caught her hand. "Thank you for this."

She smiled. "I love to cook."

He picked up his spoon and tasted his soup. "And you're very good at it. This is delicious."

"It's kind of my specialty. If you'd popped in last week, I'd have had to make French toast because I was eating cereal for supper every day."

He laughed but thinking of her coming home to an apartment as quiet as his palace and eating alone—cereal no less—squeezed his heart.

She changed the subject to the book she was reading and he told her that he'd bought his copy and would be starting it that night. "No spoilers."

"Seems to me you're not going to be starting it tonight if you're here."

"Oh, much as I'd love to stay, I have to go."

"Now?"

"I have about twenty minutes."

She laughed. "Let's not waste them."

After making love again, he returned to the palace, sneaking in the hidden back entry, parking the car in the private garage, easing through the darkness behind it and into the quiet entrance in the back of the palace.

But there, at the security desk, sat Marty Goodwin, the head of security for the palace and the entire royal family. A former military man who'd gone into public relations after his last tour of duty and eventually became a fixer for public figures, he could examine palace security from angles most security guards wouldn't even consider. Which was why he had been hired to lead palace security and manage the details of all the royals. He frequently worked nights, at this desk, monitoring the overnight shift, but also evaluating everything they had in place.

Unfortunately, tonight, it didn't feel like a coincidence that he was working the desk when Mateo had decided to sneak out.

"Good evening, Your Majesty… Have a nice drive?"

He hadn't really believed he could sneak out of his palace without his detail noticing. He simply hadn't expected to be confronted so soon. And he wouldn't apologize. He knew his parents had gone for Sunday drives and long rides to the beach—alone—while they ruled. He might not have done it before, but maybe it was time.

"I took the car I'm allowed to sneak away in."

Marty peered up at him. "You know it has a GPS locator, right?"

He stopped halfway to the back stairs, facing Marty. "No. I did not."

"Interesting thing about GPS locators, though, is that information doesn't always get checked and even if it does, there's rarely any reason to publicize it."

Realizing Marty was telling him he knew Mateo had gone to see Jessica, he took the few steps back to the desk. "No. There is not."

Marty sucked in a breath. "Your Majesty, your detail isn't charged with questioning you or judging you or even caring where you go and what you do, as long as it isn't dangerous. I would think by now you would know you can trust us and would have let us go with you."

"I'm entering new territory."

Marty laughed. "I get that and I'm sort of glad. The people you usually date seem a little phony."

"She's not phony."

Marty shook his head. "No. *She's* not. Most of us like her."

He noticed the careful way Marty avoided her name, her position at the palace or even that she worked there. "So, I have your blessing?"

"And we have your back." He returned his attention to his computer screen. "Remember that. If there's anybody you can trust, it's us. You can go anywhere you want, any time you want. We will be discreet and keep your secrets."

He knew that, of course. He'd simply never been in a situation before where he wasn't the one who would suffer if a secret leaked or the press found out. He wasn't sure Marty understood that they might be protecting him physically, but emotionally, personally, they were protecting Jessica.

"Okay. Thank you."

"You're welcome."

He walked up the stairs, torn. He absolutely trusted his security. But if push came to shove, they'd protect him, not Jessica…not her daughter.

CHAPTER ELEVEN

JESSICA WOKE SLOWLY the next morning, savoring the scent of Mateo that lingered on her pillow.

Then she realized the ringing of her phone had awakened her. Concerned that it was Ellie, she grabbed it from the nightstand and answered frantically. "Hello?"

"Did I wake you?"

Mateo.

She smiled. "No…well, maybe. I kind of drifted awake and then heard the phone. But it could have been the ring that woke me." She sat up. "What's going on?"

"I'm sorry to call you, but I am still your boss, and I need you this morning."

She eased her legs to the side of the bed, smiling at the fact that she was naked. She hadn't slept without pajamas in ages. "And I'm happy to do my job. What do you need?"

"Remember those clothes you put out for me for this afternoon's event?"

"Yes."

"Apparently, after they spent a few days on the

island dresser in my closet, housecleaning thought they were dirty and took them."

She groaned. She'd pulled them too early and left them out to justify her being gone so long on Monday morning. "I'm on my way."

"Thank you. It isn't that I can't find clothes myself. It's just that I trust everybody's opinion over my own."

She laughed. "You have enough to worry about without trying to keep up with fashion. Get breakfast. By the time you're done eating I'll be there."

"It's already ten thirty."

Her gaze leaped to her clock. "It is!"

His voice dropped seductively. "Sleep in?"

"Yes. And it was wonderful. My pillow smells like you."

He took a quick breath, and she laughed. "Hang up. I'll be there in a few minutes."

She dressed hastily and almost left her apartment without makeup. In the end, she decided to at least put on lipstick and mascara before she raced down her four flights of stairs and out into the street. Coffee would have been great, but she ignored the scent coming from the coffee shop across the street and hurried to the back of her building where her car sat.

Philip was at the palace entry when she pulled up. "Good morning, Ms. Smith."

"Good morning."

He opened her car door. "Working extra this week?"

She got out of her car. "Fashion emergency."

He laughed. "Don't let me delay you."

As Philip drove away with her car, she headed into the palace and directly to the elevator. It stopped in front of the main entry to the family's private quarters as Mateo had told her it would. But she turned right and headed down the hall to the closet/dressing room and the door through which she typically entered.

She stepped into the closet and Mateo walked in from the other side. Dressed in jeans and a sweatshirt that he'd probably worn to breakfast, he didn't say hello. He just ambled over, pulled her to him and kissed her.

She laughed. "Stop. We have serious business here. I chose your three best outfits. If house-cleaning didn't bring them back, I've got to start all over again."

"I have plenty of sweaters and trousers. Arthur purged my closet and refilled it twice a year."

She opened his deep sweater drawer. "I'm guessing he was a seasonal shopper."

He leaned on the big island dresser. "If he retires, that job would fall to you too."

She looked over at him. He'd spoken of this before. Told her she would be the perfect replacement for Arthur, but after her thoughts the night before, it suddenly felt odd. Like she didn't need to worry about losing him. They could be together forever. Or at least the remainder of his reign.

She pictured them being together like this, happy, for decades and her heart swelled—until she realized they would be sneaking around. Never out in public.

In some respects, it sounded dreamy and romantic. A secret, forbidden love was better than being the old crone in the woods, wrapped in a shawl, feeding birds—

Wasn't it?

Or was there something equally sad and desperate about being his dirty little secret? Never going to the parties he held, never having a holiday together.

"Ms. Smith?"

She shook herself back to the present. "Sorry." She pulled out a gray sweater, then walked to the closet for a blue dress shirt to wear under it. She held them against him. "Gray keeps you conservative. And the blue will look stunning with your hair."

"You know, Arthur never talks to me like this."

She laughed. "Arthur is probably very formal with you."

"In spite of being together since I was a kid, yes. He's still formal. He got worse after my coronation."

She handed him the sweater and shirt, then went searching for charcoal-gray trousers. "I think it's nice. Respectful." She glanced at him over her shoulder. "Plus, you've earned that respect."

"Thank you."

She handed him the trousers. "Should I stay and watch you dress the way Arthur does?"

He snorted. "No. But it wouldn't hurt if you chose another outfit in case this one doesn't work for me."

"Okay. Go into the bedroom and put that on while I look for something else."

"Seriously? You want me to go into the bedroom?"

"Yes! We're running out of time, and I don't want to be distracted."

He thought about that. "I like being a distraction."

She turned him in the direction of his bathroom door. "Go."

He left the room with a hoot of laughter, and she returned to the sweater drawer. She found a beautiful pale beige cashmere sweater that would probably look great on somebody with brown or red hair, but it would look plain on him.

She dug a little deeper and found a white sweater. She pulled a blue-and-white striped shirt from the closet. But she also had second thoughts about him not wearing a jacket. He was a king. A sweater might make him look casual, but she meant what she'd said about Arthur's formality being a good thing. A navy-blue blazer over his sweater really would be appropriate.

The closet door suddenly popped open. "Hey, Dad!"

Jessica froze. "Sabrina!"

"Ms. Smith?"

Mateo came walking in from the bathroom, fastening cuff links. "Hey, Sabrina. What's up?"

Sabrina looked from her dad to Jessica and back again. "I tried calling you, but you didn't answer."

The chastising tone didn't escape Jessica.

Mateo took it in stride, apparently accustomed to his daughter's moods. "You probably called while I was in the shower…"

He displayed the gray sweater with the blue shirt underneath. "What do you think?"

Jessica said, "Good. But I've decided you have to put a jacket over that."

Sabrina groaned. "You might as well have 'old man' printed on your chest."

Mateo looked at himself in one of the full-length mirrors. "I think it looks good."

Jessica presented the white sweater with the blue-and-white striped shirt. "This might be a little fresher."

Sabrina made gagging noises.

"What would you suggest?" Mateo said. "A sweatshirt and jeans?"

His daughter brightened. "I think your subjects would love it if you dressed down."

"This *is* dressing down." He glanced in the mirror again. "Besides, you're probably saying that because you want to wear jeans," he added, walking over to Sabrina.

"Yes! I'm young. I'm always on trend. You said I'm supposed to be something like an ambassador. I think dressing normally makes people relate to me."

Mateo's mouth shifted slightly in distaste.

Jessica rushed to fill the awkward moment. "Actually, I think you might have a point. It sounds like this job could be whatever you want it to be. And this seems to be your first outing…like an introduction to the position. If you dress the same way as the people you're going to see, it shows a connection."

Mateo frowned, then said, "Maybe." He took a breath. "Actually, you know what? Jessica's right. You're looking to make a connection. I *want* you to connect with the people. Not always being a formal princess, but instead dressing like a people's princess sounds like a very good idea."

Sabrina glanced at Jessica, then back at her father. "Really? You changed your mind because your *assistant* thinks it's a good idea?"

Jessica could have been insulted, but she was more concerned about Mateo's reaction. He'd said Sabrina hadn't yet grasped the concept that they served the people not the other way around. He might not take kindly to the way she referred to Jessica so condescendingly.

"I changed my mind because I realized this is your job and you're very good with people. Meaning, I should butt out. Let you define the job."

Sabrina pursed her lips, not buying one word of that. Though Jessica believed her father was being honest, Sabrina did not.

But she pasted a sunny smile on her face and said, "Thanks, Dad." She made one final scrutiny of Jessica and Mateo, her eyes narrowing, before she headed for the door. But she stopped. "Sorry. The whole reason I came in here was to find out what time we were leaving, and I got distracted." She looked at Jessica again.

Jessica combined the calculating look along with Sabrina's phrasing of being distracted and her mind hopped to a bad conclusion. She was here, on a Saturday, in Mateo's closet, as he tried on clothes and Sabrina was jumping to conclusions she shouldn't.

Glad she'd had Mateo dress in his bedroom, she eased away from him over to the closet, looking for an appropriate navy-blue blazer, getting some of the focus off herself.

Mateo smiled at his daughter. "We're leaving at noon."

"Fine." Sabrina sighed. "Wear the white sweater and blue-and-white striped shirt." With that she left, all but slamming the door behind her.

Mateo gaped at the door. "What the hell was that? I agreed with her!"

"I'm starting to get the feeling it's me she objects to."

"You?"

"I'm a woman in your closet."

"You're my *personal* assistant! Besides, I changed in my bedroom!" He drew a quick breath. "You know what? It's an hour drive to the charity. I'll have a talk with her in the car."

"Don't! I mean, you can slide in something about what a great assistant I am, making comments that are focused on my ability to do my job. But don't bring up anything else. It'll just look like we're scrambling to cover something." She winced. "Which is bad considering we do have a secret."

"Yeah, I guess." He sighed, then laughed unexpectedly. "We have a secret."

She shook her head. "Stop."

He walked over and pulled her close. "I like having a secret with you."

"In a way, I do too. But secrets can sometimes turn on a person." She caught his gaze. "We have to remember that and be careful."

CHAPTER TWELVE

ONCE MATEO WAS happily attired, Jessica left. Instead of heading directly to her apartment to clean or read, she drove to a farmer's market and chose some fruit before browsing the work of local artists displayed in booths along with baked goods and produce.

She couldn't believe what a difference a few weeks had made in her life. Getting to know Mateo, falling for him, sharing things with him, had brought her back to herself. If nothing else came of her remaining time with him, she would be eternally grateful that he'd helped give her real life back to her.

In fact, now that she was considering moving to a city, she was pondering the idea of moving to one in Brazil. She wasn't foolish enough to think that leaving Mateo would be easy—but once she wasn't his assistant anymore, their affair would be over. Rather than mope, she needed to focus on herself. Maybe restart her life. And why not move to the city where her daughter lived? In the ten years that had passed, they had pretty much become anonymous, if only because they lived simply, quietly and carefully. It wouldn't hurt to test the waters to see if they could live near each other again.

She drove home, smiling. It wasn't the perfect plan for her future, but she finally felt like she was getting closer. The crone had served her well for a decade, but she knew she needed more. She wouldn't rush to make a decision. She had weeks until Arthur returned—or didn't. Meaning, she would remain Mateo's assistant. There was plenty of time to ponder all the angles.

Right before she would have fallen asleep, her phone pinged with a text.

What are you wearing?

Mateo.

She laughed and typed, Is this your attempt at sexting?

She swore she could see him chuckle after reading that.

How am I doing?

I think we should stick to what we know. In-person contact.

Want me to come over?

She thought for a second. She wanted nothing more than for him to come over. But something tweaked in her brain. Not quite a warning, it was more of a reminder that this relationship didn't work if they went overboard. Worse, every time they met was an opportunity for someone to catch them if they weren't careful.

Sorry. Long day. I'm already in bed.

Okay.

Maybe we should discuss this on Monday? Figure some things out. Maybe make some loose plans.

That sounds good.

We'll make it good.

He sent her an LOL then texted, Okay... Goodnight.

Goodnight.

She waited a few seconds in case he had something more to say, but the light on her phone went out indicating no more texts.

She took a breath and snuggled into her pillow. Tonight, if she dreamed of him, it would be a very good dream. She would spend the next day trying to figure out places they could meet or ways he could come to her apartment. Because she really did want to take advantage of the few weeks they had left.

After that, her life would be very different. If Arthur returned, she would probably be leaving the country. If he didn't, she would be his permanent replacement, and that opened a whole new can of worms.

Sunday morning, she woke to three hard knocks on her door. Worried it might be Mateo impulsively visiting, she jumped out of bed and slid into her robe. On her way through the living room, she heard the sounds of a crowd on the street below her apartment. The coffee shop was busy, but never *that* busy. Still, she didn't have time to check.

At the door, she looked through the peephole and saw Marty Goodwin, head of palace security, with two of Mateo's regular team at his side. Confused, she quickly unlocked the dead bolt and then the simple doorknob lock.

Marty all but pushed her inside as he rushed in. "Pack a bag. We have to get you somewhere else."

"Somewhere else?"

"Our first stop will be the palace so His Majesty can explain this to you." He pointed at the window. "But until we get rid of them, you can't stay here."

Confused and a little scared, she walked to the window and saw the crowd of people in front of her building. Reporters. Some held microphones. Others notebooks. Cameramen stood at the ready, as the reporters craned their necks, trying to get a glimpse inside the glass of the building's front door.

They had figured out who she was.

Judging by the size of the crowd, it appeared they also knew she worked directly with the king.

Marty said, "This building has a basement and there's an exit that leads to your parking lot."

She faced him, heartbroken and speechless.

Marty quietly said, "We have to get going. The sooner we leave the better."

Confused, she asked, "You want me to take my car?"

"Oh, heavens no. You ride with me. I'll have someone else drive your car so it will be at the palace." He nudged his head toward the hallway that led to her bedroom. "Go pack your bag."

She gathered enough clothes for a week. At first, she thought she'd only need a weekend's worth, but the possibility existed that it might be days before this mess died down. And in that time, she'd have to resign her position. She'd have to stop working for the palace in any capacity and start looking for another job—

In another city.

Maybe even another country.

Except after this, it couldn't be Brazil.

She could not live by her daughter.

Her heart shattered. She'd been so happy. Everything had been going so well.

Maybe too well?

She would never get to live near her daughter again. Not unless she wanted to expose Eleanore to this mess. And she did not. Her own whereabouts might have been exposed. But as far as she knew Ellie was still safe.

In the car, sitting in the back seat with Marty as one of his men drove, she said, "So what happened?"

A train of cars followed them. Which was foolish. There was no way they'd get on the palace grounds.

"I've had two guards watching your apartment since you took over for Arthur. I'd been the one to vet you, so I knew your past and I recognized the possibility that some zealous reporter would dig too deep. About six o'clock this morning, my guys called in to let me know that people were gathering at the entrance to your building. Didn't take long to verify they were reporters."

"Because I'm Eleanore Smith's mother."

"That would be our guess."

"But you don't know for sure?"

"Not yet. After all, you do work directly with the king. If only one reporter was at your building, we'd assume that person had gone digging and found you. Because it's *everybody,* we know something happened."

She took a breath, saying nothing. What was there to say? Her happy life was over. She would go back into hiding, not contacting Ellie until this died down. She wouldn't bring this to her daughter's door.

They arrived at the palace and drove to the entrance Jessica always used to go to work. Marty and his team hustled her back to Mateo's office.

He rose as she entered. The look he gave her broke her heart. She couldn't let him take the blame for this.

He dismissed Marty and his guards who closed the door behind them when they left.

She immediately apologized. "I am so sorry."

He shook his head. "Don't. This isn't on you."

"But I—"

"Didn't Marty show you the video?"

"Video?" She blinked. "No. He only said that something had to have happened and that you would explain it."

"Because he's good at his job. He never oversteps."

He motioned for her to take the seat in front of his desk as he picked up his tablet and angled it so they both could see it. He hit a few buttons and a video of his daughter Sabrina popped up on the screen.

"Hey, peeps. It's me. Local princess." She smiled prettily for the camera. "It's not official yet, but I'm being groomed for a new position. The whole thing is totally bogus. Made up. Just my dad trying to make it appear that I belong, when we all know there's no real place for me in this royal family. And where did he get this idea?" She snorted. "Probably from his temporary assistant—the woman replacing his usual assistant, Arthur. When he told me about this position, she butted in. Gave an opinion that my father took. If you asked me, the woman is up to something."

Jessica's heart about stopped. Her gaze flew to Mateo. "Oh, my God."

"Keep listening."

"Seriously, not only is she overbearing but there's something weird about her." Sabrina leaned into the camera. "Like she has a secret. So, I had some hacker friends do some digging and found that her name used to be Pennelope. Pennelope Smith. Now why does that sound familiar?" She snorted in derision. "Didn't anybody vet her?"

Jessica flopped back on her chair. "Oh, my God." Shock rendered her both frozen and speechless.

"I'm so sorry."

"I'm already somewhat packed." She rose from her chair. "I'll clean out my desk."

"No! I won't let you run from this. You'll stay in one of the guest quarters of the palace until the story dies down."

She sighed and sagged into her chair. "It never dies down. Every time I think it's going to, something like this happens. I have to leave. Find somewhere else to hide. It's easier for me. I'm not the person they want. I'm merely the trail to Eleanore. But I won't have them finding her through me."

"Again, no. I won't let you leave. My daughter did this. I will handle it."

"You can't handle this! People love this story. The facts are plain as day. Why would the senator's staff have kept Eleanore at his mansion for two days except to get the drugs out of her system? Yet everybody likes to twist the story, speculate, and say what if…"

"Maybe it's time they stopped."

Her eyes filled with tears as she slumped in the chair, her body worn, tired. "I'm sorry. I shouldn't have taken this job. I should have seen what would happen when I started working directly with you. I should have realized someone somewhere would dig a little too deep—"

"And thanks to my daughter they did. But if you and your daughter were as careful as I think you were there's no connection to Ellie. There are millions of Smiths in the world. If we don't cower, don't give them anything else, they might not find her."

"I don't know… It seems risky."

"Let me put it to you this way, if you stay or you go, they have the same information. If you disappear, they can look up your airline tickets, or scan flight manifests, hoping to find times you've visited your daughter. But if you don't run away, stay here, in your little apartment, quietly working for your country, there's no connection. Hopefully, no way to narrow things down enough to find her.

"And—" He leaned across his desk. "Just once, wouldn't you like a swipe at them? The chance to tell them to get lost...with the power of a king behind you?"

When she didn't answer, he picked up the receiver of his phone and hit a button. "Pete, I want a press conference set up for noon. Those reporters want to print something? I'm going to give them something to print."

He hung up the phone and Jessica said, "I know you think you can fix this, but you can't."

"Oh, yeah? I might not fix it, but I won't let anyone tell me who I can or can't employ." He picked up the phone again. "Marty, escort Ms. Smith to the first guest quarters."

She heard Marty say, "Yes." Then Mateo hung up the phone again.

"I hope you brought something suitable for a press conference because you're coming too."

They walked into his press room to pandemonium. Every seat was filled, and cameramen lined the walls. As soon as he stepped up to the podium, the room became silent.

Mateo sighed. "Shame on you."

The hand of every reporter in the room shot up.

"Your Majesty!"

"Your Majesty!"

"Your Majesty!"

"No! You will let me have my say. First, the situation with Eleanore Smith has absolutely nothing to do with this country or my reign. So why you're concerned about her mother working for me is beyond me. Jessica was and is a normal mother. Second, Eleanore Smith was the victim. If you question that, if you fall for the innuendo that she tried to blackmail that politician and when he refused to pay she had him arrested—Answer this: Why did they keep her at that mansion for two days? That in and of itself was false imprisonment. But it also assured that the drugs used on her were out of her system.

"You're supposedly smart people. Figure some of this stuff out and stop revictimizing a woman who has been through enough."

Fifty hands shot up again.

"Your Majesty!"

"Your Majesty!"

"Your Majesty!"

"No! Stop! I won't encourage this! And Ms. Smith will not be leaving palace employ. When Arthur returns, she will go back to her usual job, and you will stop harassing her. Any outlet that pursues a story that should have been dead long ago will lose palace privileges."

He turned to walk away from the podium, mo-

tioning for Jessica to leave with him. The hands
of the reporters shot up again. A few reporters
yelled, "Ms. Smith! Ms. Smith! Don't you have
anything to say for yourself?"

She stopped. Mateo stiffened. He had handled
that situation very well, but he'd also asked her
if she wouldn't want a chance to take a swipe at
them. He couldn't yank that away from her. But
he wished he'd thought to warn her not to make
matters worse.

"Why would I need to have something to say
for myself? I'm a normal person supporting herself honestly. What is wrong with you people?
Are there not enough problems in the world that
you have to make news out of something that isn't
news? Do your jobs. Your real jobs."

She turned and led Mateo out of the press briefing room and down the hall to his office. When
they were behind the closed door, he caught her
to him and hugged her fiercely.

"You were a star."

She took a breath. "Only because you paved
the way."

He pulled back. "But you got the chance to have
your say. That was important."

"Yes."

"Now, we have to deal with Sabrina."

She shook her head. "No. *You* have to deal with
Sabrina."

"You can't run from this either. It's a power

thing. If she believes she intimidated you, she'll use it. I watched both Olivia and Josh go through it. Hell, I did it myself. Testing out my power as a royal. She hasn't yet learned that ruling by fear makes everyone an enemy."

"That's probably exactly what you should tell her."

He laughed. "Agreed. Then I'm going to ground her. The way I should have when she flashed at the club. I'm also going to make her shadow Josh and Olivia for a week."

"Oh, I'll bet they're going to love that."

"I don't care. I might have created this problem with her by letting her get away with things or not being around enough. But I intend to fix that while she's grounded. She'll be at *my* side too. She'll eat most meals with me. Play chess with me. Go riding with me. Until we find that common ground where we can talk for real and get to the bottom of this."

CHAPTER THIRTEEN

BECAUSE IT WAS SATURDAY, Mateo's kids all had plans for dinner. Except for Sabrina, who had received the lecture of her life from her father and was grounded. In an attempt to protest, she refused to come down to dinner and he sent her a note that said, "Fine."

Knowing he'd be alone with Jessica, he'd had the chef make steak Florentine with Brussels sprouts, roasted potatoes and red peppers because he knew it was one of her favorites.

He knew a lot about her now. Silly, frivolous things like her love of pancakes, warm, cozy blankets, and antiques, furniture and accent pieces that had meaning. But tonight, she looked forlorn after their long day, especially since she could not call Ellie. He had to cheer her up.

"When we're done with dinner, I can give you a tour of the palace."

She sighed. "Thanks, but I'm tired."

"You're not curious about the paintings or vases that date back to the seventeenth century or even the gifts given to us by dignitaries from other countries. We have a whole room full of those things."

She laughed softly. "Are you about to show me that you live in a museum?"

"No. With the exception of artworks of note, all those things are in one big room." He frowned. "I guess that *room* is like a museum."

"And I guess I might like to see it."

He snorted. "Might?"

"All right. I really would."

"You know with your love of things from the past, wonderful paintings, and furniture used by dignitaries, you should have been the royal."

She peeked up at him. "No. You're doing just fine. You were like a school principal with a bunch of bad kids with those reporters this morning. You didn't try to defend me. You told them they were off base rehashing old news."

"No, you were the one who reminded them it was old news." He chuckled. "I think the guy in the third row peed himself."

"Don't even!"

"Ech. He's new. The other reporters probably went back to their offices, weighed the pros and cons of opening up a story that really is ten years old and decided it wasn't worth their credentials at the palace…and he followed suit."

"With a sigh of relief."

Mateo nodded. "With a sigh of relief."

Nevil served dessert—chocolate cake with chocolate frosting and whipped cream. To his credit, he didn't miss a beat or change his expression while serving the entire meal, but Mateo saw the sympathy in his gray eyes. Nevil had been around almost as long as Arthur and he knew working for the royals wasn't all peaches and cream.

But the sympathy in his eyes also showed how much Nevil liked Jessica. He saw her nearly every morning at breakfast and knew that she worked hard. Like Mateo, he appeared to see the injustice in the way Jessica had been treated.

Tossing his napkin to the table, he said, "Ready for that tour."

"Considering that I'm staying here for a while, how about if we save the tour for someday when I'm less tired."

"Okay… Then I'll just walk you to your room."

"No need. Marty took me there this afternoon, along with my luggage."

He pulled out her chair, took her hand and nudged her to stand. "I'm walking you to your room anyway."

"But—"

He put a finger to her lips to stop her. "My home. My rules. Plus, the staff you see here today are very loyal. No one will say anything."

"I guess there's no law against walking a woman to her room."

He snorted. "Exactly. But I thought maybe we'd watch a movie."

Her gaze flew to his. "Really?"

"It's my daughter's fault that you're upset. Therefore, it's my responsibility to entertain you enough that you can fall asleep."

They found a movie they both wanted to see and sat together on the sofa in the sitting room of her suite. She nestled against his side, and he put his arm around her. Memories of Sabrina's mean-spirited video drifted off into nothing, along with the press conference and her worries about her daughter. She didn't have to say it. He could feel it in the way she relaxed against him and laughed at the silly movie they'd chosen.

He wasn't happy that she'd endured what she had that day, but he was unbelievably touched that she turned to him, trusted him. He wasn't surprised. They had a genuine emotional connection. But he'd also never felt this with another person. The honor of her trust.

This time when they made love it cemented something. The thought that he would lose that something rent his heart. Without even knowing, he'd waited his entire life for her and in a few weeks, she'd be leaving him.

The following morning, he awakened in her bed and groaned.

She sniffed as if slowly pulling herself out of her slumber, then her eyes opened, and she bolted up in bed. "Oh my God! We slept in."

He winced. "And with each other."

He expected her to commiserate. When she started laughing, he gaped at her. "What part of this is funny?"

She stole a quick peek at the clock on the bedside table. "If you want to make it to breakfast on time, you're going to have to do the walk of shame."

"The what?"

"Walk of shame. You know, a person stays out all night with a lover and then somehow they have to get back in their house. Or pull their car into their driveway without the neighbor seeing them. Or climb up the stairs of their apartment building before the guy next door comes out to go to work. Or in this case, sneak back to your quarters without anyone seeing you in the same clothes you wore yesterday."

"You're lying there all smug, but this doesn't reflect well on you either."

"Why? I slept with a really handsome, extremely sexy guy last night."

"Yeah, well I slept with a gorgeous woman—"

"Not the same. I get a lot more street cred for sleeping with you than you get for sleeping with me." She stretched up off her pillow to kiss him. "Clock's ticking, Your Majesty. The longer you stay in this room, the more chance someone will see you. Or that you'll be extremely late for breakfast…when one or all of your children could ask why."

Disgruntled and just wanting to stay with her, not have to race around starting his day, he eased out of bed and began yanking clothes off the floor.

Jessica said, "If it's any consolation, I thought last night was worth it."

"Probably because you're not about to be caught."

"There is that. But I meant what I said about you being handsome and sexy."

He paused, enjoying the full force of her compliment as it rolled over him. She always knew the right thing to say at the exact moment it would have maximum effect, mostly because he knew she meant what she said.

He remembered his thoughts from the night before, when he'd felt something cementing between them. Not just a click of connection or a sense of rightness. More like forever.

After the unified front they had to present the day before, the thought didn't surprise him as it usually did. But he decided that was because they were getting close. Closer than he'd ever been to another person. Yet he hadn't forgotten their relationship wouldn't last. Realistically, with Sabrina's latest stunt in the disastrous video, it was clear just how eager the press would be to find Eleanore Smith, while Jessica wanted her to stay hidden. He knew she would move heaven and earth to keep her daughter safe if they began getting close to finding her.

Even if she didn't have to disappear for her

daughter's sake, Arthur could decide to come back, and she would return to the assistant pool, where seeing her would be next to impossible and personal time together would be nonexistent.

So, no. He and Jessica did not have a future.

He looked at her, still snuggled in the ornate bed of one of his glamorous guest suites and his heart shimmied. He loved seeing her in his home. He thought of dancing with her the night before the ball for Josh's birthday and knew she had loved getting a taste of his life.

He wanted to give her all of it. But he couldn't. He could only make the best of the time they had.

"What would you think about me hosting a ball for the employees?"

She blinked. "A ball just for employees?"

"Considering there are at least two hundred including security, office staff, maids, cooks, motor pools, groundskeepers, I think it would be fun."

Holding the sheet against her chest, she sat up. "It would be wonderful."

"We wouldn't be giving tours of the palace. But everybody would see that corner of it." He sat on the edge of the bed. "I could mingle, meet everyone." He frowned. "You'd probably have to give me a study sheet, so I'd know who everyone was and where they worked."

"But they'd get to meet you." Her face shifted from surprised to pleased. "I think everyone would love it."

He squeezed her toes beneath the thick floral comforter, undoubtedly one of the ones he'd nixed for his own room. "And we could have a dance."

She gasped. "Are you sure that's a good idea?"

"I will dance with as many people as I can so that my dance with you blends in."

"I could wear a gown with a big skirt that would swish when we waltzed."

He got up from the bed. "Sounds like a plan."

She smiled. "It does."

"And you're in charge."

She pressed her hand to her chest. "Me?"

"You'll get plenty of help from the kitchen and waitstaff." He bent down and kissed her. "Plus, I think you'll have fun doing it."

He took his clothes into the bathroom to dress. When he emerged, she was up and dressing too. He caught her around the waist and kissed her, happy with his plan of hosting a ball for her. But misery quickly filled him. No matter how many things he squeezed into the next few weeks, his happy affair with the most wonderful person he'd ever met would end. She'd be gone from his life. And he'd be lonelier than he'd ever been because he now knew what he was missing.

She pulled back and grinned at him. "Good luck getting to your quarters." She turned to go into the bathroom but faced him again. "Oh, and some people don't put on their shoes when they sneak out so they can be stealthier."

He looked at her, studying her face, memorizing the color of her eyes, the way her hair looked disheveled from making love with him the night before. "Now, I think you're just pulling things out of thin air."

She laughed. "Go ahead and think that but if a board creaks when you step on it and somebody hears you, don't blame me."

She walked into the bathroom, closing the door behind her and his heart actually ached. Still, he had work to do and a breakfast he couldn't be late for. He glanced at his shoes. If a person had to make the walk of shame shoeless that might be part of why it was so shameful.

He carried his shoes anyway and was relieved when he saw no one in any of the corridors. He also had the advantage of the entry through his closet, which cut down the amount of time he was in public areas. All pitfalls navigated, he made it without being discovered.

He showered and dressed and arrived at the breakfast table to find Olivia and Josh.

Pulling out his chair, he said, "No Sabrina?"

Josh winced. "She's pretty angry with you."

He gaped at him. "She's angry with *me*?"

His daughter and son looked at each other. Olivia clearly spoke for both of them when she said, "Honestly, Dad, we're a bit confused. Was Ms. Smith not vetted?"

"Of course, she was vetted. Of course, we knew

who she was. But…" He glanced from his son to his daughter. "Think it through. Did she really *not* deserve a job because of something that happened to *her daughter*? And when Arthur took his leave, were we supposed to overlook her when she was next in line for the position?"

"I understand what you're saying," Josh put in. "But you have to admit she is a lightning rod for controversy."

"Which is confusing since her daughter's situation was ten years ago," Mateo said reasonably. "No one would have even known who she was had your sister not decided to use her hacker friends to investigate her. In a roundabout way, she's the one who broke the law."

"Oh, really?" Sabrina said, sashaying into the dining room. "Eleanore Smith's mother might not have broken any laws, but she obviously has your ear. You take her advice. And that's dangerous."

"No, it isn't! I took Arthur's advice too. A personal assistant is supposed to offer observations and advice about family, about what I wear, about what should be served at state dinners… There's a lot of things I need her advice for."

Sabrina took a seat. "She went too far."

Mateo just stared at her. "She always saw your side of things and that made you angry?"

"The two of you were just a little too chummy."

"Clearly, you forget how close Arthur and I are.

Do you know he's called me three times a week on this sabbatical he's taken?"

Sabrina mumbled, "No."

Josh winced. "He's called me too, checking up on you."

Mateo pointed at his son. "See? A personal assistant is more like a friend than an office mate."

Sabrina said, "Whatever. I still don't trust her."

"Then you're in for a world of trouble because if Arthur resigns, we're offering her the job." He glanced at Olivia. "Do *you* have a problem with her?"

Olivia sighed. "No. Honestly, she does the job as well as Arthur. She caught on as if it was second nature to her. There wasn't as much as a ripple in the way you handled your days."

"Josh?"

He shrugged. "I saw the same thing. She's smart. She stays quiet."

Sabrina snorted.

Josh glared at her. "She does! I think part of your problem might be that you're the one who forgets decorum. You barge into Dad's office. You barge into his quarters—"

"He is my father."

"She's right, Josh." He looked at Sabrina. "I don't mind you coming into my quarters or my office. But you do have to respect my systems. Having an assistant who is with me in my office and at breakfast...who chooses my clothing...buys gifts for dignitaries…reminds me to drink water and runs interference with staff…is a huge help to me. And she's doing a great job."

Sabrina rolled her eyes. "If you overlook the fact that her daughter is questionable."

"Sabrina, her daughter is not questionable."

"How do you know! My God, Dad! No one even knows where Eleanore Smith is. Innocent people do not hide."

"Innocent people who don't want to be hounded by the press have no choice but to hide."

Sabrina threw her arms in the air. "There is no talking to you! You don't simply take everyone's side but mine; you also ignore my advice…which, in this case, might be extremely valuable."

Bouncing up from her seat, she stormed out of the room.

Silence reigned for thirty seconds. Mateo took a breath. "If you two agree with her about Jessica's daughter being some sort of security risk, there is no time like this minute for you to say so."

Olivia quietly said, "I understand why her daughter hides. One misconstrued comment can live in the press forever."

"Actually, Olivia, Eleanore simply wants a normal life. It isn't just the press that questions her, it's bosses, neighbors… She's had to change her name."

Josh said, "And you know this because?"

"Because Jessica and I spend from eight to twelve

hours together every day. We talk. Just as I knew everything about Arthur's family, I know about Jessica's daughter. There is no more story there. And, if anything, working for *us* potentially hurts Jessica more than she could ever hurt our family."

Josh winced. "That's true. Sabrina investigating her might revive her story and send reporters looking for her."

Olivia shook her head. "We are the trouble here."

Mateo took a breath. "Yes. We are. That's why Jessica is staying in the palace for a few days. And God only knows what will happen after that." He said words that stuck in his throat, hurt his chest, as a horrible realization hit him. "She might leave us. She might have to walk away from everything that's in her apartment and disappear so she'll be gone before anyone even misses her. Before the press has a chance to realize she's on the move."

Olivia dropped her head to her hands. "Ugh. We're terrible."

"Not us. The life we live. We are the lightning rods. Not her."

Josh said, "Do you think she's just going to leave one night… Not tell anyone?"

The thought went through him like an arrow, and he realized that what he'd felt while they made love might not have been a cementing of their connection as much as desperation. Passion that shot through them because they both knew they didn't have forever. "I'm hoping not. I'm also trying to think of ways to fix this."

Olivia pondered that. "We could give her that little guesthouse behind the vegetable garden."

He thought of how Jessica had wanted to live in a cottage in the woods and almost smiled. She'd never leave before the employee ball, if only because she had a responsibility to plan it. But the house behind the vegetable garden would be a good way to keep her protected, and yet give her some space until then. But he couldn't say what would happen after that.

"We could make the offer."

"If she can't ever leave the property," Josh said, "wouldn't that be a little bit like a prison?"

"Maybe she could stay there until the noise dies down?" Olivia suggested.

Mateo gave voice to the horrible thought that had been on his mind since Jessica had said it. "If the noise ever dies down. With us being part of the story, it gets new life." He picked up his napkin as Nevil entered the room. He quickly asked for eggs and bacon and Nevil scurried to the kitchen. "Until it fritters away, I'm keeping Jessica preoccupied planning a party for the palace employees."

"A ball?"

"When we had to inspect the ballroom for Josh's birthday party, Jessica told me she had never been in that part of the palace. She told me no one she worked with ever had."

Olivia and Josh looked at him expectantly. "And?"

"And we don't know any of the people who work for us—who serve us—beyond their jobs. They are all extremely competent people who are loyal, and we vet them, make them sign confidentiality agreements, want their undivided loyalty, then all but ignore them."

Josh frowned. "That's true."

"While Jessica is living here, rather than have her focus on hiding out, I suggested we hold a ball for employees that she planned. That way she won't have time to worry or overthink things."

Olivia caught his gaze. "You've certainly thought this through."

"It is our fault she can't go home."

Josh said, "Agreed."

Olivia said, "I'm all for it." Finished with her breakfast, she rose and kissed her dad's cheek. "You have a very soft heart." She smiled at him. "A good heart."

He caught her hand and squeezed. "You do too. You'll make a wonderful queen."

Josh rose too. "Well, my *pragmatic* heart and I are going to work. I'll see you both later."

Mateo waited for Jessica in the dining room for fifteen minutes after he'd finished eating. When she didn't show up, he made his way to his office where he found her at her desk. "You didn't come to breakfast."

She winced. "Sorry. Was I missed?"

"We talked about you."

She sighed. "That can't be good."

"It wasn't really bad either. I got to ask Josh and Olivia the obvious questions. They support you. Sabrina does not. But, honestly, the bottom line to her ranting was that she wants me to hear her opinions. She thinks I don't pay attention to her because I never do what she wants. Which is ridiculous. She left breakfast in a huff, but she's grounded, so I'll have a talk with her tonight. I'll explain that the two of you aren't competing. That you fit into certain roles, and she fits into other roles. But when it comes to what clothes I wear or what I send to foreign dignitaries as gifts…your opinion rules. And when it comes to philanthropic things, her opinion will rule."

Jessica thought about that for a second. "That sounds good."

He sighed with relief. "Thanks. Actually, after her performance at breakfast this morning, I finally saw where I went wrong with her." He ambled into the room. "Her brother and sister are so much older than she is that I forgot that they've been easing into their duties for years. They've been attending meetings, conferences and negotiations as observers since they were eighteen, and now they look perfect for their positions. But I sort of dumped Sabrina into her role the day that we visited the Eliminate Hunger warehouse. I need to find a way to ease Sabrina in too. Maybe take her to more of my charity events, introduce her to people…with her knowing that someday she will be in charge of this end of our duties, the way Josh and Olivia knew they would someday run parliament and the kingdom."

"That sounds perfect!"

"I hope so." He paused for a second then said, "Olivia also had an interesting idea."

"She did?"

"Yes, she suggested we give you the cottage behind our vegetable garden to live in while you're staying with us. We can't let you go back home until at least some of this dies down but the cottage would give you a sense that you aren't living at work."

"It does feel a bit strange to be here all the time."

"I can take you back there but before I do, I think we should meet with the master of the household and at least pick a date for the ball."

"That would be great."

They designated Friday four weeks out for the ball. Jessica was thrilled to be planning it, but a wisp of melancholy wove through her as she and Mateo met with the master of the household and made a skeleton outline of the night's events. Arthur should be returning the Monday after the ball. In a way, that night would be like her Cinderella moment. She'd get to dance with her handsome king, but her time with him would be over.

With the bare-bones idea for the ball sketched out, Mateo rose. After he dismissed the master of the household, he faced Jessica. "Let's go look at the cabin. We won't take any of your things over until we're sure you like it."

She nodded. "How could I not like a cabin behind a garden. It sounds perfect."

"Yes, but if you've never actually lived in a house that is behind a huge garden and in front of a forest…it might surprise you. Especially the wildlife."

She winced. "I've actually only ever lived in cities."

He laughed. "This should be interesting."

He led her down a corridor, then another that took them to a sunroom. Plants filled every available space where there wasn't a sofa or a chair.

"This is beautiful."

He opened the back door. "Let's hope you feel the same way about the cabin."

They walked down a cobblestone path that wound through flower gardens filled with buds and blossoms that had been started in a greenhouse and now filled the space with color. That morphed into vegetable gardens where young plants were beginning to flourish.

She looked around in awe. "This is huge."

"We like our fresh vegetables."

Beyond the vegetable garden was a patch of grass like a front yard and beyond that was a cozy little house. She approached cautiously. "It's pretty."

"And I called ahead to have housekeeping come in and give it a quick dust and change the linens while we talked about the ball."

She faced him, knowing her eyes probably shimmered with happiness. "Thank you."

"I know how hard it is to work where you live… so—" He shrugged.

"You came up with this idea?"

"Olivia did."

She laughed, fighting the urge to take his hand and lead him up the wide front porch with two wicker chairs and a small table…a good place to have morning coffee.

When they stepped inside the house, it was as charming as the vision that she'd had for the cottage she'd believed would be her sanctuary. A thick sofa and matching chair were angled toward a stone fireplace. Hardwood floors were partially covered by fluffy rugs. Vases of flowers were everywhere.

"It's lovely."

"I'd offer it to you forever, so you'd always have the protection of the royal family. But Josh reminded me that after a while it could seem like a prison."

She faced him. "You know that the three of you are quite a team, right?"

"Yes."

"And now you're going to add Sabrina to that mix."

"Slowly."

She laughed. "Every time you take her to an event is a chance to talk to her, draw her in." She smiled, realizing he'd probably planned it that way. "Damn. You really did think this through."

"She's my daughter. I want her to be happy and to fit in."

"I feel the same way about Ellie. I just want her to fit in. It isn't that she hides, but she does look over her shoulder. Keep her past to herself. She'll never have a normal life…not completely. She was offered the job as head of public relations for the real estate company where she works but she had to turn it down…even though her degree is in PR."

"Why'd she have to turn it down?"

"It involved going to events, doing interviews with the local paper when the company was expanding, being in ads that were televised. That kind of thing. Though she desperately wanted it, it was too much exposure. So she stayed an agent."

"She still has to meet people, be around people."

"Yeah. But it's local people, one-on-one. Her name's never in the papers. She doesn't do television commercials." She sighed. "She still talks about how she hated not being able to take that opportunity."

"The unexpected consequence."

"Of someone else's actions," Jessica agreed. "That one night totally changed her life."

He glanced around the small cabin. "So do you think you could be happy here for a few weeks?"

She nodded. The reminder of their limited time brought her back to their own problems. Mateo might not understand that these could be their last weeks together. She didn't know if he realized Arthur could be returning the Monday after the ball.

But she knew Arthur hadn't filed papers to officially retire or even discussed it with human resources. True, he might make a last-minute announcement, but Arthur wasn't a last-minute kind of guy. He was a planner. The way things looked to her, he would be coming back to his job—

And she would be ready. She wouldn't pout or be sad, but she would miss this. Their casual conversations. Their easy connection. She knew she'd never find this with another person. And when the time came, she'd be even lonelier than she'd been when she'd lucked into this job.

Because now she knew what she was giving up.

CHAPTER FOURTEEN

THE DAY OF the ball arrived with the palace buzzing with excitement. Given that it was a party for the employees, including the kitchen and waitstaff, the event had been catered. Security was being handled in rotating shifts so that all the guards would get to attend the ball for a few hours with their spouses or dates.

Jessica decided to dress for the event in the guest suite in the palace so she wouldn't have to walk up a cobblestone path in a gown. A member of palace security had gone to her apartment to retrieve the red gown she had worn to her ex-husband's Christmas parties. She brought her makeup and toiletries with her to work that morning and set them up in the guest suite bathroom before she went to breakfast.

By late afternoon, everything in the palace sparkled and glittered from a recent cleaning. The scent of good beef, roasted potatoes and sugary baked goods filled the air.

She made her last inspection of the ballroom

then headed to the guest suite to dress. The security guard had been instructed to lay her gown on the bed and she went directly to the bedroom to make sure it was there. But when she walked in the room, her red dress was not on the bed. Instead, a big white box with a huge yellow ribbon sat on the floral comforter.

Seeing a card under the bow, she walked over and retrieved it.

This is your night. I bought you the dress you'd told me you wished you had.

Mateo

She slid the ribbon off the box and opened it to find a purple satin dress. When she lifted it out, it swelled around her, and she realized it was the dress she'd said would fan out when they twirled while waltzing.

Her heart squeezed and tears filled her eyes. For thirty seconds, she asked the universe why she'd met him, why she'd been allowed to fall in love with him, when there could be nothing permanent between them.

Then she realized that she'd so very casually admitted to herself that she loved him, and she fell to the bed.

She loved him.

She loved him.

Not in the "I'm content" way she'd loved her husband, but with passion and hope. Commitment. She'd do anything for him, and she knew from the gown sitting on her bed, he'd do anything for her too. She wasn't simply a convenience to him or a number on a to-do list or someone he sneaked to the cottage to sleep with every night. He saw her. He respected her opinion.

They were a perfect match. If her life and her daughter's life were different, she would leave everything for him. With him, she could face the life of being his queen, if only because they would be in it together. She longed to be the one who could support him, advise him. She longed to be the one who could keep him sane when there was trouble. She longed to be the one who filled the needs no one else knew he had.

She just wanted the chance to love him. Everything he was. For real.

The futility of all these wonderful feelings closed her eyes in despair, but she popped them open. She refused to wallow or wonder why. They might not be able to be together forever, but this time with him had been a remarkable gift and she intended to enjoy this night.

She showered, put on makeup, did her hair, then slid into the gorgeous gown. She didn't know how he'd figured out her size or even where he'd gotten the dress, but she didn't care. She knew security was aware of their affair, but every damned employee in this palace could wonder about their relationship. It didn't matter. In another day or two, she'd be gone.

Mateo might think she was going back to the assistant pool, but she couldn't. She could not work in his palace and pretend there was nothing between them when she loved him enough that she'd give up her plans and be his queen.

Every day would be torture. She would have to leave.

A knock sounded on her door, and she lifted the full skirt of her gown to race to answer it. When she saw Mateo, she caught his arm and dragged him into her room the way she had the first time he'd visited her apartment.

"What are you doing! Anyone could see you out in that hall!"

He closed the door with his foot, then pulled her to him and kissed her. "You look amazing. I knew you would…and I didn't want my first glimpse of you to be in front of everyone where I couldn't enjoy it."

She fanned out the big skirt of the gown. "It is beautiful." She caught his gaze. "Thank you. I will remember this forever."

Mateo loved her thanks, but he hated the finality of her words. Saying she'd remember the dress forever was the first piece of admitting their time together was coming to an end.

"This is a night for fun. Not a night for thinking." He kissed her. "Let's go downstairs."

She raised her eyes to meet his gaze. "Together?"

He winced. "We can walk together so far. Then my arrival has to be announced with trumpets. I'd love to have you walk in with me, but I'm pretty sure you don't want any part of that."

She could picture it. Because they belonged together. But it wasn't to be. So, she faked a laugh and answered the way he expected her to. "No. I do not."

"Fine. I'll walk in with Sabrina or Olivia the way I always do." They headed for the door, but he stopped her. "You do remember that you're hostess for this, right?"

"I thought I only planned it."

"That makes you hostess. You're like the liaison between the royal family and the guests. They'll be more comfortable with you anyway, so it's up to you to make them feel welcome. You should stand at the main entrance and greet them. If you want a receiving line of a sort, get Pete and Molly to join you. They are also well-known and liked by staff."

"That would be really nice. Thank you."

The urge to kiss her was so strong that he had to fight it. But he looked at it as practice. For the rest of the night, they would have to behave the way they did in the office. Not the casual, comfortable way they were in her cottage. Two lovers who wanted nothing more than to spend precious time together.

They took the stairs to a common area, where

Jessica veered to the left and he headed down a hallway to a small room where the royals gathered before all major events in order to enter together.

Josh had brought a date. "Dad, this is Irene Corsicovia." He turned to his date. "Irene, this is my father, His Majesty Mateo Stepanov."

Wearing a strapless peach gown that acknowledged the warm weather, and looked perfect with her red hair, Irene curtsied. "It's a pleasure to meet you, Your Majesty."

He bowed slightly. "It's a pleasure to meet you too." He frowned. "I think I know your father."

"You do, Your Majesty. He owns several vineyards throughout Europe."

Mateo smiled. "I am acquainted with him and his wine. I hope he and your mother are well."

"They are, Your Majesty."

Olivia arrived, also with a date. Glittering in a white gown covered in crystals, she said, "Dad, this is Raymond Daher. Raymond, this is my father. His Majesty Mateo Stepanov."

Raymond bowed. "It's a pleasure to meet you, Your Majesty."

"The pleasure is mine," Mateo said. His heart warmed at the way Raymond and Olivia held hands like people in a serious relationship and Josh stared adoringly at Irene. His children were growing up, but more than that, he could picture Jessica fitting into the intimate family scene. A scene where he, Olivia and Josh were simply people, not royals. Just a dad meeting the love interests of his two adult children.

Sabrina arrived alone, but for once she wasn't angry. With her dark hair piled on top of her head in fat curls and sparkling green eyes, she looked so pretty Mateo began to realize just how beautiful she was. But sometimes beautiful and reckless spelled trouble. She'd spent the past four weeks grounded for outing Jessica in the video, but he'd been drawing her into his charitable duties, hoping she'd begin to see her role and some of her anger would dissipate. While she did very well meeting people and understanding the place of philanthropy in their kingdom, she continued to be grumpy and moody. Still, he blamed that on the boredom of being grounded.

They entered the ballroom as three couples. Olivia and Raymond were announced first. Josh and Irene were second. He and Sabrina were third. He'd asked Olivia, Josh and Sabrina to prepare remarks acknowledging and thanking the staff. Olivia's thank-you became a toast that nearly brought down the house with applause. Josh's was a little more sedate and also showed that he very clearly knew who worked where and that he appreciated them.

When he faced Sabrina, she shook her head slightly, indicating that she had not prepared anything. Not surprised, Mateo simply rose and went to the podium.

"Well, this party is certainly long overdue."

The crowd applauded. Someone whistled.

"I know that my life is busy, and the loss of my beloved queen made my private life difficult… but these past few weeks, working with Jessica Smith has shown me that in a lot of ways, you are my family."

The applause erupted again. More people whistled.

He quieted them with a motion of his hand. "I've always known just how much you do for me, but these past weeks talking with Jessica, I've realized you might not know how much I appreciate all that you do.

"I'm not going to give you the it's-lonely-at-the-top speech because I know I am blessed. But I'm also blessed to have each one of you. I'd like to make this appreciation ball a yearly thing."

The applause began again, but this time he raised his champagne glass in toast. "I could not be as efficient of a leader as I am without you. Salud."

With that, he motioned for the band to begin the dancing. As always, he danced the first dance with Sabrina. It was a tradition begun after her mother's death that continued on as she grew up. And now, here she was, a young lady. Suddenly, he could see a bright future for her, and he knew instinctively that the day would come when she'd see it too.

"Thank you for the dance."

She smiled. "It's tradition now."

He laughed. "Yes, it is."

"Until you find someone."

He searched the statement for a double meaning, or a hint that she knew about him and Jessica, but found none. "It might be a while given how busy I am."

She giggled and patted his arm. "Poor Daddy."

The words hit him right in the heart. They transported him back in time to when she was a very happy little girl. His heart swelled with love.

"Anyway, I think the ball was a great idea and I'm looking forward to meeting the staff."

That took him by surprise, but he didn't let that show in his expression. Her steps might be shaky and inconsistent, but she was growing up. He said simply, "As am I."

The music stopped. She curtsied and he kissed her cheek, then she blended into the crowd.

For the first time in weeks, he had the sense that he didn't have to worry about her. Then he glanced around the room, looking for Jessica. But remembering that he was supposed to be dancing with other women to take the attention off them when he danced with Jessica, he tried to find likely candidates to dance with.

Having memorized the spreadsheet Jessica had created for him, complete with employee pictures, he moved into the crowd. The first person he found was the executive suite receptionist, Molly. Glad that the first person he ran into was someone he knew, he happily invited her to dance, and she accepted.

After that dance, he joined a group of his security detail, who were hanging out at the bar. The people who would be taking the next shift and the one after that were abstaining from alcohol, but the group that had just gotten off duty had ordered beers.

He drank a beer with them, then found the head of housekeeping and asked her to dance. After the dance, he mingled with people who were still seated at tables.

Half a row in, he ran into Jessica. Literally.

She laughed. "Pardon me, Your Majesty."

He instinctively caught her hand. "No. It was my mistake. Not looking where I was going."

He fought the instinct to kiss her knuckles. "Since we're already here…how about a dance?"

"That would be lovely."

He guided her to the dance floor, but the band played a fast song that prevented him from really dancing with her and didn't allow for the flare of the skirt of her ball gown.

When the song was over, she curtsied and scurried away.

Disappointment shuffled through him. But he continued his plan of dancing and mingling.

After the band's first break, Arthur and his wife approached him.

A tall, slender man with white hair, his former nanny, current personal assistant, caught him in a huge hug. His wife curtsied, but Mateo laughed and hugged her.

"We're like family."

"As you said in your speech."

"Yes," he agreed, "but the three of us were family before that."

Arthur looked down at his champagne glass then up at Mateo. "Thank you for this."

Mateo tilted his head in question. "For the ball?"

"Yes. You have the most dedicated staff in the world. They appreciate being acknowledged."

"I'm sorry it took me this long to figure that out."

"Rumor has it that your temporary assistant Jessica might have instigated this."

He snorted. "We were here, doing the Friday night inspection for the ball for Josh's birthday, and she mentioned that most of the staff hadn't ever seen the ballroom, and some hadn't ever even been on the executive side of the palace."

"That's true."

"It hit me that it shouldn't be that way."

"I'm happy you saw…and I think Jessica does get the credit."

Mateo chuckled. "She moved into your job remarkably well."

"I'm so glad. It was good to be able to recover in peace." He glanced around. "But I'm fine now. Not just recovered but rested and ready to take my job back."

Mateo was surprised. But Arthur was very good at what he did and probably the most loyal employee in the palace, which was saying a lot. The job was his and he was well enough to return to it.

"It will be good to have you back."

"Monday morning, the usual time?"

Mateo reached out and shook his hand. He said, "The usual time," happily but his chest tightened. Jessica would go back to the assistant pool, and now that a month had gone by since Sabrina's disastrous social media post he also suspected she would move back to her apartment.

Arthur and his wife drifted away, and Mateo stood on the sidelines, disappointed that his one shot at dancing with her had been a dismal failure, until it finally dawned on him that he could ask the band to play a waltz. He walked up to the lead singer and made his request then went back to mingling again.

When the band played the familiar chords of the waltz, he found Jessica in the crowd, and she found him. Too far away to hear each other, he didn't say a word. He simply smiled at her.

They walked across the dance floor and met in the middle. Enthusiastic couples joined them, and they blended in like the other attendees. Just two people enjoying the dance.

Their gazes caught and held as the music swept them away, the huge skirt of her gown flaring out behind her.

When the music stopped, his heart hurt. He had finally fallen in love. It was so much deeper and richer than he ever imagined but it was wrong. Pointless. Again, he was struck by the injustice of it. Worse, they were in public. He couldn't kiss her, tell her he loved her—

He couldn't say or do anything.

They drifted apart slowly, with Jessica smiling like the perfect employee. He smiled like a happy boss. No one would ever guess there was anything between them.

It was a foretaste of what his life would be without her. With Arthur coming back, even if he ventured into the assistant pool, this cool, efficient version of Jessica was all he'd ever see.

Marty Goodwin scurried through the crowd and caught Mateo's arm. "Your Majesty! Sabrina has been in an accident. She's at the hospital." He twirled Mateo in the direction of the door. "We need to take you there now."

Jessica ran over in time to hear Marty say, "We need to take you there now," and followed them, saying, "I'm going too."

Swiftly moving through the crowd, Marty said, "There's no reason—"

Mateo stopped dead. He might not be able to kiss her or tell her he loved her, but right in this minute, he needed her. "She's going."

Marty said, "Of course, sire," and hustled him and Jessica through the crowd which had stopped dancing and stood in a weird, suspended animation.

From the corner of his eye, Mateo caught Josh taking the microphone from the band's lead singer. Clearly having been briefed, he told the attendees to continue dancing. "Sabrina's been in an accident, but she's fine. Everything will be fine."

From the slight shimmy in Josh's voice, Mateo didn't believe that.

CHAPTER FIFTEEN

THEY WERE RUSHED through a private entry of the hospital and whisked up to a private floor with security at every corner. The guards didn't surprise Jessica; neither did the secure entry, or the entire floor being designated for the royal family. What shocked her was the décor. The nurse's station looked like a small office. The floors were gorgeous hardwood. There were no numbers or markings on the doors. The place looked like the bedroom area of the palace.

A man in green scrubs met them halfway down the hall. "I'm Doctor Ford, Your Majesty, the physician who saw Sabrina when she was first brought here by ambulance. Your daughter was in an automobile accident and her left leg was broken. She's being taken to surgery and is expected to make a full recovery."

Jessica pressed her hand to her chest, grateful it wasn't as bad as it could have been.

Mateo said, "Thank God."

Dr. Ford motioned them to walk into a room

with sofas, chairs and a television. Jessica glanced around again. Everything was so perfect, it could have been a sitting room in the palace. Quietly luxurious.

"I'm sorry, Your Majesty, but you'll have to wait here."

The doctor left and Marty entered the room slowly as Jessica and Mateo lowered themselves to one of the sofas.

"Details are sketchy, but we've been told that Sabrina was riding with a friend who was driving drunk."

Mateo shook his head. "She was at the ball."

Marty took a long breath. "We think she must have taken advantage of one of the times when the guards at the gate were changing shifts." He sucked in another breath. "If you'll pardon my forwardness, Your Majesty, nothing gets by Sabrina. Knowing she wouldn't have a detail assigned to her at the ball, she could have had this planned or simply seen an opportunity and taken it. The gentleman she was riding with was also at the ball. His injuries were less severe and he's fine."

"Thank you, Marty."

He bowed slightly. "If that's all, sire, I'd like to check on the security downstairs and then return to the palace."

"Yes. Thank you, Marty."

The door closed behind him and the waiting

room became quiet. She caught Mateo's hand. "I'm so sorry."

"The doctor said she's expected to make a full recovery."

"Yes. But it's still hard."

He blew his breath out on a sigh and rose to pace. "Where did I go wrong with her?"

"You didn't. She's eighteen. She's been grounded for weeks. She's probably bored silly. She saw an opportunity and took it."

"With a guy who was drunk?"

"Maybe he didn't look drunk? Maybe she didn't think far enough ahead to even wonder if he'd had too much to drink." She shrugged. "You told me that you had your share of 'normal' moments when you were young. Didn't you ever take a foolish risk?"

He looked at the ceiling. "Yes."

She rose and walked to him. "I know this is upsetting. But you have to keep your wits about you. Technically, she's going to be stuck at home for months because of this. You could tell her that she extended her own grounding by sneaking out. You could also tell her that Fate isn't always kind...or fair. That she's been lucky until now, but things won't always break her way." She paused long enough to be sure he was paying attention. "But that's a talk for when she's feeling a bit better."

He squeezed his eyes shut. "Yes."

She took his hand and led him to the soft couch

again. "Now that we're clear on that, I'm going to give you permission to be a normal dad. To pace. To worry. To get all your confusion out while you're alone with me. So no one has to see it. Especially not Sabrina." She winced. "At least not yet."

He sat. "Okay."

She sat beside him. "For the next couple of hours just be a dad."

He nodded.

Her heart went out to him, but she was overwhelmingly glad she was there. Not just to support him but to help him respond correctly with Sabrina. This was the role she was born to play. His helpmate. It couldn't be forever. But she was here now, and she would be whatever he needed.

She took a breath, looked at the solid door that separated them from the rest of the world and laid her head on his shoulder.

He'd been there for her. She was here for him.

Hours later the surgeon came in and explained the procedure they had performed to realign the broken pieces of the bone. The prognosis was good, but he intended to keep Sabrina in the hospital for at least a week, maybe longer, depending on how she was healing. Full recovery would be four to six months.

"She'll be out of post and in a private room shortly. You can see her then." He glanced at the king's tux and Jessica's ball gown but didn't mention their attire. He simply said, "I'll be in my office for another hour or two, Your Majesty, in case you have questions."

When he left, Mateo felt his first relief in hours. She really would be fine, and she was about to be trapped at home, to heal, for months.

He turned to Jessica. "You're right. She certainly extended her grounding. There's a lesson there."

"Something you can use when she's well enough to have the discussion about her behavior," Jessica agreed, pulling out her phone. She went to contacts and he heard the beeps of the phone dialing.

"Marty? This is Jessica. Would it be possible for you to have someone from your team get jeans and a sweater for His Majesty?"

Mateo said, "Have them get something for you too."

"Have them go into the cottage and grab jeans and a sweater for me too."

She disconnected the call and smiled at him. "I have a feeling you're not going to leave. This way we're good until late tomorrow."

He ran his hand down his face. "Thank you."

"That's my job, remember?"

He did. But the things she did didn't feel like obligations or even thinking ahead to help him the way an assistant would. They felt personal. Like this is how the person in his life would be a partner. They'd think of things for each other, do things for each other. Not just perform roles, and handle mandatory tasks, the way he'd spent his entire life.

Except with his kids. He'd always been real with his kids. Jessica had seen that and stepped in with good advice so he could keep it that way.

His heart began to mourn her loss again, but he stopped it. She was here. Now. And he was beginning to understand why people lived in the moment. Sometimes it was all they had.

The following afternoon, Sabrina was recovering well enough that Jessica and Mateo returned to the palace. When the driver pulled up to the entryway, he faced Jessica.

"There are a few things we need to handle in the office, if you don't mind."

"Of course, not, Your Majesty."

They exited the limo and the guard at the door opened it for them. At first, they went in the direction of the office, but he took the quick left that led to the back stairway to his quarters.

Climbing the steps, he caught her hand. Her heart bumped against her chest. They were holding hands in a common area. Of course, Sabrina was in the hospital. Josh now had a girlfriend he spent time with, and Olivia rarely came over this way.

And security knew about their relationship.

There wasn't any reason to panic.

He led her into his quarters through the closet and she laughed. "I know you've been under a lot of pressure, but you're going to get us caught."

"Nope. I made that up about having to work so no one would be expecting you to leave and after a while they'd forget you were here. You're going to do the walk of shame in the morning."

Another laugh escaped. "Not if I don't fall asleep!"

He stopped, faced her. "Yeah. That's a better plan."

"I still have to walk outside to get to the cottage."

"Not if you stay in the guest quarters one more night. No one would question that."

"Huh. You're right." They walked through the bathroom into his bedroom and when he stopped by the bed, she said, "You've been planning this."

"A king doesn't host a ball for the woman he loves without wanting the chance to show her that he loves her."

Her heart shimmied. "Don't say that."

"It's my country. I'm pretty much allowed to say what I want."

With that he kissed her and every nerve ending in her body melted. He was the love she'd waited her whole life to find even though she didn't know she'd been waiting.

They undressed each other slowly, as if they had all the time in the world, and she understood why. They didn't have all the time in the world, so they had to memorize every important second. This time right now might be the most important memory they'd make because he'd told her he loved her.

She didn't just love him. He loved her too.

They fell to the silky sheets beneath the comforter. Their gazes caught and held as he ran his palms along the curve of her torso. Her breasts nestled against his chest. Their legs tangled.

"Have I ever told you you're beautiful."

"You might have mentioned it a time or two."

He laughed. "You are."

She didn't want them talking. There was too much chance they'd slide over into forbidden territory. She'd spoken to Arthur at the ball, knew he was returning on Monday and she didn't want to get stuck on how awful it would be to lose each other. She wanted the raw, earthy passion of two people desperately in love.

Her hands cruised down his chest, as she eased up enough to kiss him. She put everything she had into the kiss. Not just to keep him too busy to talk but to ignite the kind of fires he always lit in her. She loved the feel of him, strong muscles under smooth skin, peppered with dark hair, and wouldn't let herself think any further than the moment.

He rolled her to her back, kissing her greedily, igniting burning sensations deep within her. Then he eased his lips from her mouth to her breasts, fanning the flames until every inch of her tingled with need. As if feeling the same things she was, he separated her thighs with his knee, and they came together in a storm of passion that left them both breathless.

Afterward, they whispered in the dark, though she doubted anyone could hear them even if they shouted. She wouldn't let him slip over into the conversation that haunted them both. Not only had the weekend been difficult for him, but there was no point to discussing their future.

They had none.

When he fell asleep, she redressed, then picked up her shoes and laughed.

It seriously would not be the walk of shame if she wasn't carrying her shoes.

Laughing through tears, she headed into the bathroom, then the closet, then the extremely quiet corridor. She walked down the hall to another set of steps and quietly climbed them to the floor with the guest quarters.

She almost took a shower but didn't want to risk ruining the warm glow that filled her. He loved her. No thought, no words, had ever been so wonderful.

After a good night's sleep, she showered and dressed to return to the hospital. Right before she would have texted Mateo for instructions, he told her he would be at the limo waiting for her. They would eat breakfast at the hospital.

When they arrived, Sabrina was asleep, so Mateo went to the nurse's station to make sure they had alerted her doctors that he was there and ready for an update on his daughter's condition.

Phone in hand, Jessica took a seat on one of the chairs of Sabrina's quiet room.

"I really screwed up this time, didn't I?"

She carefully glanced over to the bed where Mateo's youngest child lay, her leg in traction.

"That's not for me to say."

Sabrina snorted. "You never hesitated to give your opinion before."

"I don't counsel you. I counsel your dad. If he were here and you said that, and he looked to me…then I would give my opinion. That's my job."

She grimaced. "That's what my dad said. But I know he's probably furious with me. And I might need help."

Jessica said nothing.

Sabrina groaned. "Come on. Throw me a bone. Tell me what to say to him."

"Ohhhh…no! This is all on you."

She sighed. "Yeah. I get that."

Jessica turned her attention to her phone, but curiosity got the better of her and she glanced at Sabrina again. "Let me ask you something. Was sneaking out of that ball all about needing to be out? Or was this a power trip? You know…showing your dad that no matter what he said or did, you'd find a way to do what you want."

"I'd been cooped up for weeks! I needed to get out!"

"Oh, poor you. Cooped up with a chef and swimming pool and a gym and tennis courts and horses and beautiful gardens."

"It's all boring!"

"Is it really?"

"Yes!"

"What do you do when you go out that's not boring?"

Sabrina shrugged. "I don't know. Talk. Dress up. Take rides. Dance. Have fun."

"You could have danced at the ball."

"Maybe."

Jessica suddenly saw what was going on. "You *were* proving a point."

Sabrina said nothing.

"You know that ball was in appreciation for all the people who work in your palace, and you left. Your actions said that you could not care less about the people who serve you. Did you even talk to anyone?"

When Sabrina stayed silent, Jessica shook her head. "Your dad adores you. He'd give you the moon, yet you always find ways to rebel like nothing you have is good enough. Have you ever once said thank you or that you were sorry when you pulled one of your stunts?"

The door swung open, and Mateo walked in. "Hey, you're awake."

Sabrina shifted on the bed. "Yeah."

He walked over and kissed her forehead. "Feeling better today?"

"A bit."

He turned to go to a chair, but Sabrina caught his hand. "I'm sorry."

He smiled at her. "We'll talk about that later."

"No. Really, Dad. I'm sorry. I didn't think about anything but the fact that there'd be a chance I could escape. I didn't think about anybody but myself."

"You know, the friend you talked into driving you to freedom was arrested."

She squeezed her eyes shut. "No."

"Things you do have consequences, Sabrina. Being a princess doesn't protect you from life or promise you anything. You have to grow up. Maybe even faster than a normal kid does. Because that guy's life is forever changed. You can walk away from this. He can't."

Her eyes filled with tears. "I'm so, so sorry."

"And you have four to six months of recovery time to think through how you need to change."

Several of Sabrina's friends asked for permission to visit her. Mateo did not grant it. First, she wasn't recovered enough to have friends. Second, she was on enough pain meds to believe she could get out of bed and try to escape…again.

He and Jessica stayed all day Sunday, and Sabrina slept on and off, proving she wasn't yet ready for company. At nine o'clock that night, she was so sound asleep that Mateo decided it was time to go home.

They walked down the hall holding hands and he didn't even realize it, until they met the security detail that walked them to the door to the private area of the parking garage. If either one of his guards noticed, they said nothing. It wasn't their job to comment or criticize. Their job was to protect him. They escorted him to the sedan, opened the back doors for him and Jessica, then slid into the front seat to drive them back to the palace.

They stopped the car in front of the entrance Mateo typically used. When the back door opened, he began to slide out, but she stayed where she was.

When he glanced over his shoulder at her, she said, "I'm going to the cottage tonight."

He nodded. "Okay. I think we can actually work tomorrow morning. We'll do breakfast then go to the office and handle the things that can't wait so we can go to the hospital in the afternoon."

She smiled slightly. "Have you forgotten Arthur will be back tomorrow?"

He paused. The air changed. This was it. The

end. Worse, it felt anticlimactic. The end of the most wonderful love affair of his life was his beloved telling him his old assistant would be returning.

His emotions rebelled, but in all the weeks they'd been together, he hadn't been able to divine a way they could have forever. If anything, his thoughts always hit roadblocks. And the roadblocks weren't nuisances, or inconveniences or even problems that could be solved. They were futures. Both Jessica and her daughter had rebuilt their lives from the ground up. He couldn't destroy that or ask them to roll the dice and take a risk that having Jessica marry into a royal family wouldn't bring a shower of press down upon them. After Sabrina's post that gave away Jessica's identity, there'd be no way.

"Does this mean you'll be in the assistant pool tomorrow?"

"I guess. I'll have to see HR."

"Maybe come to breakfast first? Fill Arthur in on what's been happening?"

She hesitated. "If you feel we need the transition?"

Relief filled him. "I do."

"Okay. See you at breakfast tomorrow."

CHAPTER SIXTEEN

MATEO'S SECURITY DETAIL drove her to the door of the cottage, and she thanked them before she ambled into the little house. Someone had lit a fire to take the chill out of the air. She suspected Mateo had instructed his security detail to handle it, but her chest tightened.

She'd never been so in sync with anyone...or so in love that she'd happily be the woman by his side forever, give up her simple existence to be his queen, if it were possible. But it wasn't. Monday, with Arthur returning, her final breakfast would be all about handing over her duties.

The thought of it broke her heart and filled her eyes with tears. Especially since Arthur probably didn't need to be brought up to speed. He'd done this job forever.

She'd be a redundancy—

She would no longer be Mateo's assistant. She would be a nameless, faceless employee in the assistant pool again.

Her head filled with images and ideas of how

the following week would be. She wouldn't even see Mateo in passing. There would be no sneaking around because if they were caught there was no built-in excuse.

When Sabrina had outed her to the press, she'd agreed to stay in the palace and then the little cottage because her job kept her protected by palace security. Now…she would be an ordinary employee. No specific duties. Only requests from executive staff. Arbitrary jobs. No continuity. No position. Just jobs—

No one would miss her if she didn't show up the next morning. Technically, she could go home.

She took a breath.

She could go home.

She could go anywhere.

And maybe that was the thing to do.

Go. For real.

Get on with the rest of her life.

Not tomorrow. Not the next day. Right now.

Deep down inside she'd always known this was their breaking off point and a wise woman would accept that. She wouldn't hang around and pine over someone she couldn't have. She wouldn't spin fantasies about how things "might" work out.

She would recognize truth and move on.

She walked back to the bedroom to repack her suitcase with the clothes she'd brought with her the day security had scooped her up. She also had a lot of things at her apartment that she would want to retrieve. Technically, her rent was paid for a month. The smart play would be to leave now, find a new home—probably in another country— and return to pack for real and have everything shipped to her new apartment.

It seemed like such a good plan that she didn't consider that she'd been through a difficult weekend with Mateo and Sabrina and she might not be thinking clearly. She didn't consider the emotions connected to losing him. She simply acted. She finished packing her bag and called security. In less than an hour, she had made flight arrangements, and a guard was driving her to the airport.

Mateo arrived in the dining room the next morning finally feeling refreshed. The only way he could have felt better would have been if he had slept with Jessica, but knowing Arthur was returning she'd already drawn the dividing line.

So, he'd stayed up a good bit of the night, fighting the urge to call her until he had the answer to how they could have a relationship. For real. Forever. As always, he couldn't think of one, but he wasn't done trying. He'd fallen asleep out of exhaustion and slept surprisingly well. This morning, he would update Arthur on his duties and the clamoring staff who would want to see him, and he would text Jessica and tell her that he refused to believe they couldn't work this out.

He would text her every twenty minutes until she agreed with him.

He felt so good about his plan that he ordered blueberry pancakes.

Arthur arrived, electronic tablet in hand. "Good morning, Your Majesty."

"Good morning, Arthur. It's good to have you back."

Josh entered. "Arthur! You're back."

"Yes. It's good to see you, Prince Josh."

Josh took his seat. "Are we able to visit Sabrina yet?"

"She was very good yesterday. Still a little loopy from drugs, but I think you and Olivia can go any time you want. Together or separately."

Olivia arrived and took her seat. "We can finally visit?" She glanced across the table. "Hey! Arthur!"

"Good morning, Princess Olivia. I trust you slept well."

"Very well." She looked at her dad. "And I'm eager to see Sabrina. You and Jessica were all the company she had since the accident. She's probably ready for a good conversation."

"You wouldn't have been able to talk anyway. She slept on and off all day Saturday. Yesterday was better." He zeroed his gaze on his daughter. "Do not overtire her."

Olivia smiled demurely. "I'll be fine." She looked around. "Speaking of Jessica…where is she? Does she just go back to the assistant pool? I mean, now that she's trained in our inner workings, it might be good to keep her in the executive suite. I could use a good assistant."

"You have an assistant."

"Meh. I think I'd like Jessica better."

It twisted in Mateo's gut that they were talking about Jessica as if she were a commodity instead of a person. To his family, she was only an employee when to him she was everything. But he couldn't say anything. He needed to talk to Jessica, get her to admit she would stay. Then he'd talk to his kids…

Then…

Well, he didn't know what. But he could not believe his relationship with her had to end.

"Shall I read today's schedule?" Arthur asked.

Mateo's blueberry pancakes arrived. "Let's wait for Jessica."

Arthur frowned. "Security's docket from last night indicates that she was driven to the airport around midnight."

Mateo stopped cutting his pancakes. "What?"

"She left, Your Majesty. I thought perhaps she'd needed a small holiday after her stint as your assistant and that she'd given you a date she'd be returning."

He set his fork down. "No. She did not mention that to me. But I'll look into it."

"*I'll* look into it," Arthur corrected. He shifted

his gaze to the tablet. "Your first call this morning will be to the hospital to check on Sabrina. Then you have two meetings you can't miss. But after that I'm canceling everything so that you can spend the afternoon at the hospital."

And just like that Mateo's world returned to the one he'd had before Jessica. When breakfast was eaten and they entered the office, Arthur immediately went to his desk to get the hospital nurse's station on the line, and confusion shimmied through Mateo. He felt like he'd fallen off a cliff and landed back in time. His weeks with Jessica became a weird memory, something so good he must have imagined it.

As if she didn't exist.

Jessica arrived in London late that morning. She'd basically slept on hard plastic airport chairs and on her flight. Having visited London, she knew a good, reasonably priced hotel and got a room. As soon as she was settled, she took out the burner phone she'd used to call Ellie when she'd first moved to Brazil and dialed her daughter.

"Mom? Why are you calling on the burner?"

"Are you kidding? After that mess with Sabrina, I wasn't going to risk the press tracing my calls."

"What mess… Are you talking about Princess Sabrina? I didn't think your work at the palace involved her."

Remembering that she hadn't told her daughter about her promotion to Mateo's assistant, she sat on the bed and slipped off her shoes.

"Get ready for a long story."

She told her daughter about the promotion and Sabrina's obvious dislike of her as the king's assistant, then the mess with her hiring hackers to dig into Jessica's past and the social media post telling the world she was Eleanore Smith's mother.

Ellie gasped in horror. "Are you kidding me?"

"No. The king held a press conference and more or less shamed the reporters for even wanting a ten-year-old story."

"That must be why there was nothing about it in the press here." She paused. "I also didn't see anything on social media."

Jessica eased up to the headboard of the bed and curled against it. "Maybe Mateo really did shame them into letting the story die."

"Mateo?"

She took a breath. "You don't work as someone's *personal* assistant for eight weeks without getting a little personal."

Eleanore laughed. "Oh, really?"

"Stop. I will admit it was fun having a handsome king interested in me—"

Ellie's gasp came through the phone. "He was *interested* in you?"

"We were interested in each other."

"Mom! You…you… I don't even know what to say."

The thought of her weeks with Mateo filled her with warmth and she laughed. "It was yummy. He was…is…so handsome and thoughtful and his first marriage had been arranged so I felt like I was his first love, and he felt like mine…"

"Mom! You scamp! You seduced a king!"

Jessica said, "Stop!" through her laughter. "The thing of it was our relationship would have been nothing but trouble. Royal families are always objects of the press. Your story would be magnified if I'd added a royal romance."

"Magnified?"

"Anybody who gets involved with someone in a royal family can expect to have their life dissected. That's actually why I called. I left my job and my apartment. I'm in London. I think I'll live here for a while. You know…maybe until I retire. Then I can get that little cottage in the woods." The sense of boredom about the cottage hit her like an avalanche. She'd somehow let go of that dream to include Mateo in her life and could even see herself as his queen. Now she was back to being the crone in the garden, who did nothing but read and knit. The shift almost gave her a headache.

Not ready to think about that, she ignored it. "Anyway, let's use the burners for a while, then we'll see where we stand."

"Okay." Ellie drew a deep breath. "But something feels off about using the burners. Wrong. I mean, when I first moved to Brazil these phones were like a lifeline. And moving around was almost normal. Now, everything feels off. Especially you leaving Pocetak."

Surprised, Jessica said, "You're just feeling that because we haven't had to move or hide for a while. Neither one of us has."

"You might have moved but you never left Pocetak. You never really hid the way I had to and—I don't know—Today it all feels wrong." She took a breath. "Why did you leave Pocetak?"

"Because of Sabrina's social media post. She outed me. I couldn't stay."

She didn't have the heart to admit she also couldn't bear to see Mateo on the news, in the papers. Even now, the thought of never seeing him again made her chest hurt.

Still, she was strong. Smart. She would get through the pain of losing him.

"Okay. I guess I understand."

Ellie might understand but Jessica heard confusion in her daughter's voice.

But this wasn't the time to talk about it. They could sort it out once she was settled. "I'll be apartment hunting tomorrow and once I find a place I'll make one more trip back to my old apartment to box things up and have them shipped there. I'll get a new phone and send you both that number and my new address."

Ellie quietly said, "Okay."

Jessica's heart splintered. She knew it had to be difficult to move to a different country, stay away from friends… Only talk to her mother by phone.

But there wasn't another way.

"Right now, I'm going out for some food then I'll take a long shower and get some sleep."

"Okay. Goodbye, Mom."

"Goodbye, sweetie."

Her day went exactly as she told Ellie it would. She got food and a shower and then went to bed. But when she woke the next morning, and opened her phone to apartment hunt, she didn't have the sense of urgency or excitement she'd had the other times she'd moved. She'd been with the palace for years. Been in her apartment for years. Without Sabrina's interference, she could have stayed there forever.

Thoughts of Sabrina became thoughts of Mateo, and her breathing slowed. They'd been together ten or twelve hours a day for eight weeks. They'd flirted, danced, made love, ate breakfasts together. And now he was just gone from her life, as if a magician had snapped her fingers and made him disappear—

She stopped those thoughts. She would get beyond this. She always did.

But memories bombarded her. Especially dancing with him at the ball, in a dress he'd bought for her because he listened when she talked. But their quiet, private moments had been better. Right from the beginning she'd realized she could confide in him, and he could confide in her.

And today, his daughter was in the hospital. There was no doubt she'd recover, but he was alone. In a way, he was always alone.

She squeezed her eyes shut, absorbing the pain of knowing in her heart of hearts that she was supposed to be his mate. His helper. His lover. As he was supposed to be hers. She believed she was the answer to some silent prayer he'd made—maybe even decades ago.

But she couldn't be. Their stars did not align. Her being with him would expose Ellie.

Friday, Mateo went to the hospital at one o'clock in the afternoon as had been his practice all week. Sabrina was awake but grouchy. Which was how he knew she was coming back to normal. He found her doctor and spoke with him about letting her go home and what preparations would be necessary.

The list wasn't long, but it was specific and not for the first time that week, he'd wished Jessica was still his assistant.

But deep down he knew he didn't want her around to be his assistant. He wanted her in his life as his partner. And that couldn't be.

He asked the doctor to have the nurses print the

instructions for his staff, then he walked back to Sabrina's room.

"I just made arrangements for you to come home."

She sat up awkwardly, trying not to move the leg in traction. "You did?"

"Yes. But there will be rules. There will be a nurse in your quarters at all times to make sure you're not doing anything physical beyond what you are allowed to do."

"Okay."

"And I will allow visits from friends but one at a time."

She swallowed as if preventing herself from saying something, but ultimately she agreed. "Okay."

"For someone who was grouchy when I came in, you're being very accommodating."

"I'm beginning to realize I was more than a little self-centered. That you were a really great dad and I took advantage of you."

He laughed. "Really? And you're going to change?"

"Jessica sort of told me I had to."

His heart twisted at the mention of her name, and he realized that was part of his sorrow. No one even said her name anymore. She was gone in a puff of smoke, and he seemed to be the only one who remembered her.

"What did she say?"

Sabrina shrugged. "Just something like I pushed

you or pushed your boundaries or something."
She shrugged again. "The part I remember was
that she asked me if I ever told you I was sorry
for things I did. And that's when I started to see
things from your perspective. I didn't stop to realize I always made trouble for you."

He could almost see Jessica speaking to Sabrina
honestly, firmly, but not yelling. Just throwing out
breadcrumbs that his daughter clearly followed to
a good conclusion.

"If you mean that, I might let you have two visitors at a time."

She laughed. The sound was like music to his
ears. Jessica had done that. Put her on the right
path.

His heart broke all over again.

"I know you liked her."

His head snapped up.

"She liked you too. What I can't figure out is why
you let her go."

"It's complicated."

She snorted. "That's what people say when they
don't want to be honest."

"I can be perfectly honest, but you might not
like it. You're the one who brought attention to
her daughter through your shenanigans with the
video."

She sighed. "I was just mad."

"Yeah, well, your outburst had consequences.

Her daughter who is hidden probably got harassed—"

He paused. He didn't really know what had happened.

Sabrina said, "Did the press come after her?"

He thought about that for a second. Weeks had passed between the video and his press conference and the ball. No one had shown him any repercussion articles. No one had even mentioned it again.

It was as if it was irrelevant.

Of course, he'd never asked Jessica. Lots could have been going on behind the scenes—

No. She would have told him. That was the kind of relationship they had.

"I think you should go after her."

He sniffed. "You? *You* think I should go after your nemesis?"

"I might have been a bit hasty. She's pretty nice."

"She's very nice. Very kind."

Sabrina grinned. "Very pretty." She sobered. "Go after her, Dad. I'd never seen you act the way you did with her. I'm going to feel really awful if you go back to being all stuffy like Arthur."

He laughed. They spent the rest of the afternoon talking about her schoolwork and her potential place in the kingdom. This time, he didn't act as if it was a done deal. This time he made her understand that she was young, that neither her sister nor her brother had taken their place. They were both in training and it might be decades before Olivia was crowned queen and decades before Sabrina would be experienced enough to head up a department.

The sun had set by the time he summoned his detail and returned to the palace. Tired, missing Jessica, he ambled into the entry foyer. Marty Goodwin manned the main station just inside the door.

"Good evening, Your Majesty."

He stopped. Since the employee ball, things were a lot more personal between him and staff. "Good evening, Marty."

"The updates I'm getting from the guards at the hospital indicate that Sabrina's doing well."

"We're bringing her home tomorrow, getting nurses, a hospital bed...that kind of thing."

"We'll be on top of it."

"I know you will..." He turned to go but stopped and faced Marty again. "I know security took Ms. Smith to the airport, but did anybody by any chance find out where she was going?"

Marty gave Mateo a strange look. "She was a member of the palace staff. We always keep track of staff for a few months after anyone leaves just to make sure they aren't selling state secrets."

Mateo frowned. "Stealing secrets?"

"No one's ever done it, but it's protocol. We follow up on everybody. Anyway, we checked flight manifests and discovered she went to London."

"London?"

He shrugged. "We'll follow her employment history, learn where she's living…until we're satisfied that she didn't leave with confidential documents." This time, he laughed when he said it and Mateo laughed too.

"I know you're not kidding but I can also tell you think it might be going overboard to keep tabs on her."

Marty shook his head. "I have a sixth sense about these things. She's a good person. She won't be writing a tell-all book and she didn't take documents. But it's protocol to follow through. Better safe than sorry."

He nodded. "Good night, Marty."

"Good night, Your Majesty."

Mateo walked to the back stairway, his heart pounding in his chest. She'd gone to London. He loved London. He'd love to be in London with her.

Who was he kidding? He'd love to be anywhere with her.

Sabrina's questions about Jessica's daughter and the press popped into his brain and he turned and went back down the stairs.

"Marty, Sabrina asked me today if there were any repercussions to the stunt she pulled with the video, outing Jessica. I know your team is always doing threat assessments. Was there a problem?"

Marty hit a few keys on his laptop. "There was chatter on social media. There always is. A few podcasters brought it up." He scanned his screen. "It looks like the security people who listened to the podcasts reported that comments ran in Jessica's daughter's favor."

"Really?"

Marty laughed. "There was a general theme that people should just let her alone." He glanced up at Mateo. "I wouldn't say there would never again be interest in the story or that she'd never be hounded again, but if there was ever a time for someone to come out of hiding and give an interview, this might be her daughter's."

Ridiculous hope grew inside Mateo. Given Marty's background, if anyone knew how to navigate these waters, it would be him. And if he was right about Ellie not hiding anymore, there was a chance for him and Jessica.

Marty said, "When we look at something like this situation from a public relations perspective, there are two ways to handle it. The first is to hide, which is what Eleanore Smith has been doing. But the second is to confront the situation outright. To dare anyone to challenge or disagree with you. That's actually how a security team can bring a lot of enemies out of the woodwork. It's how we identify the real problems."

Mateo frowned, thinking that through. Having Ellie do a press conference that challenged her enemies would be the risk of all risks and not something Jessica and her daughter would agree to. Not after this many years of relative peace.

"Of course, you don't hold a press conference just to say I dare you to confront me to my face. There has to be some substance behind your motivation. A message."

Mateo said, "Such as?"

"If Jessica's daughter did an interview that said her situation was the worst time in her life but it's over and everyone could learn a lesson about trusting the wrong person from her story...she'd probably earn a lot of respect."

That sounded empty and insubstantial. "And that's it?"

Marty bobbed his head. "A lot of people can bring victory out of a bad situation by starting a nonprofit to help people who have been in a situation similar to theirs. In Eleanore Smith's case, I think the focus of the group could be a legal fund to help victims get justice." Marty caught his gaze. "To start and run a nonprofit like that, she'd have to have money though. Lots of it."

Mateo's heart stopped. A nonprofit could more than give meaning to Jessica's daughter's heartbreak. It could start her on a new path. Bring her out of the shadows and give her back her life.

"What she needs is a backer." He stepped away from the security desk. "Jessica told me Eleanore works in real estate in Brazil, but she was trained in PR."

"PR is a very good thing to know when you're running a nonprofit. She could be the voice of the company. Then I think she'd have to hire lawyers, therapists, social workers, counselors."

"Exactly. Now, we just have to see if she's interested. Ready to come home and take the lead on this."

"If she's half as strong as her mother, I'm guessing she'll jump at the chance."

Mateo headed for the stairway again. "Call my pilots. I want to be in London first thing tomorrow morning."

CHAPTER SEVENTEEN

JESSICA HAD BREAKFAST in the hotel, then spent the morning looking at apartment listings, making notes. Everything was so expensive, she had decided to expand her search farther away from the city when a knock sounded on her door.

Thinking it was probably someone from housekeeping, she walked over and said, "Who is it?"

"It's me."

Mateo's voice sent unexpected happiness careening through her, then confusion, then fear. He couldn't stand in the ordinary hall of an ordinary hotel in a huge city where half the population could recognize him on sight!

She yanked open the door and dragged him inside. "Is your security team about ready to throttle you yet?"

He laughed, but he also kissed her quickly, then ambled into her room. "This is nice. A little simple, but nice."

"This is what normal people can afford."

"So, you're back to normal?"

Her face scrunched. "I've always been normal."

He laughed. "Sort of. After you left, Sabrina and I had a talk about her video."

She winced.

"She's extremely repentant and she actually asked if there had been any repercussions, and I realized I hadn't heard anything about her video. Security tells me Ellie was mentioned on a few podcasts and there was some social media chatter... but nothing serious. Almost as if no one cared."

"Ellie said she never heard anything about it either." Confused, she followed him to the small table in her room and offered him one of the two chairs. "Actually, Ellie hadn't even heard about the video at all."

He didn't sit. He stood a few feet away, looking tall and handsome and also normal. In his baseball cap and jeans, he wasn't a king. He was just the guy who made her heart melt.

"No news outlet reported it?"

She told her melting heart to settle down, that he'd clearly come to discuss Ellie's situation, maybe even to help her. No smart person turned down an offer of help from a man with genuine power.

"Not in Brazil."

"So, maybe what made it newsworthy in Pocetak was the fact that you were working for me?"

She thought for a second. "Yes. I think so."

"Which means, it was your connection to *me* that made it newsworthy."

Not sure what he was getting at, she nodded. "Yes."

"Which also means that anyone who has a relationship with me...whether it's a business association or a personal relationship is going to endure some scrutiny."

Now truly confused about where he was going with this, she was ready for him to explain himself. She crossed her arms on her chest. "What's your point?"

"I miss you."

She hadn't been expecting the conversation to become personal. He'd shifted gears so quickly that she didn't have time to stop the swell of longing that rode through her. Still, it was pointless for them to pine for each other, and they both knew it. "It's only been a few days."

"Six. And six days is a long time to miss someone."

She didn't know whether to laugh or commiserate. It almost seemed as if he didn't know how to handle the loss.

"It *is* a long time. But we both knew this was coming."

"What? Arthur returning to his job or you stealing out in the middle of the night?"

She winced. "It seemed like a good idea at the time. Everything happened so fast that leaving felt like a clean break."

"It was a horrible thing to do." He sighed. "Arthur was the one who told me that your drive to the airport had been on Sunday night's security docket. No one at the breakfast table seemed to be concerned. Everyone took it as you needing a few days away after spending two months as my assistant and you'd gone to London for a little break." He sighed. "So, there I was, upset because you'd left and not able to show it let alone process it."

The sadness in his eyes touched her heart. Duty had kept him from focusing anywhere but on his role as king. But he'd never been in love. Never had his heart broken. It was no wonder he couldn't process it. "This really is all new to you, isn't it?"

"It's not all new to you? You weren't upset?"

"Of course, I was upset."

"Then why did you leave?"

"Because we don't work as a couple. I can't be in your life. You can't be in mine."

"Two months ago, I agreed with you. Especially as our relationship potentially affected your daughter—brought her back in the spotlight. But with the lack of response after Sabrina's video, I'm not so sure anymore."

"You're telling me I should take what I want and to hell with my daughter?"

"I'm saying maybe it's time to stand up for yourself."

"Stand up for myself?"

"And for Ellie to stand up for herself. The two of you needed some time to pass quietly after her assault and the trial that was more like a circus. Now ten years have gone by. You're stronger. She's stronger. Maybe it's time to look the reporters in the eye and tell them that that's all behind you now."

She wanted to be indignant, but he'd told her as much before their press conference and Ellie had almost come to that conclusion in their conversation. Still, right now, it wasn't so much what he was saying that made her heart speed up and her stomach tighten. It was why he was saying it. He hadn't come to London, dressed down and sneaked into her hotel room to give her advice about her daughter.

He'd missed her so much he'd been thinking about her situation, trying to find a way to make it all work out. The magnitude of it didn't escape her.

"I do not want to lose you." He took a breath. "I do not want to live without you."

She licked her lips, not sure if she was afraid or overjoyed by what he was about to say.

"I want you in my life forever and if that means we have to address this once word gets out that we are romantically involved, it seems like a small price to pay. Maybe even time for Ellie to have a normal life."

Fear and longing collided. "Oh, my God. You want me in your life for real and you think that's a normal life?"

"It is for me."

She squeezed her eyes shut. Hope and happiness begged her to just say yes. She'd thought about this the whole time they were lovers. Longed for it. But she was older, wiser and experienced enough to know bringing Ellie out of hiding meant real trouble.

Yet, she wanted him. So desperately wanted him in her life forever, that she wished his optimism had merit.

"This isn't going to be as easy as you seem to think."

"I don't care." He sucked in a breath. "I love you. I have never felt this way before. I don't want to feel it with another woman. I want you."

"Is this a royal command?"

He snorted. "I could make it one. But I'd rather have you just be a woman with me. Not a royal. Not a subject. Not even someone who sees me as her king. Just a woman who loves me as a man. A woman who would share my public life but who would want me for myself…a guy with kids and an exercise regimen, who loves to ride horses and sometimes gets headaches and longs for the day he can sleep until noon. I've never felt like a king with you. Just a man. I never knew how good that could feel or how important it was until I met you and now, suddenly, I can't live without it." He caught her gaze. "My life, my needs have changed since I met you."

"You should be me. I wanted a quiet cottage in the woods. I wanted my daughter to be happy. That's all I wanted. Now, I want to sleep with you every night. I want to talk about our kids as if they are *our* kids. I want to be the person you tell your secrets to, the person who is by your side when you rule. I want to wake up to the sound of your voice."

"You love me too?"

She nodded.

He caught her hands. "It would not hurt if you said it."

She laughed through her tears. "I love you."

"Then we are going to make this work."

He kissed her then and she let herself melt with happiness and also the sense of destiny that always lived on the fringes of their time together.

He pulled back. "There is one more thing."

She winced. "I hope it's not another warning about what life with a king will be like."

He laughed. "No. I had a conversation with Marty and we got to discussing your daughter's situation from a security/public relations standpoint. He thinks if we start a nonprofit that's a legal fund to help victims it would bring Ellie into the spotlight but as a leader. Not a victim, but someone changing the world."

She thought for a second. "Oh, my goodness. She would love that."

"She definitely loves it. I called her last night. Midnight our time is only seven o'clock in Brazil."

Her eyes bulged. "You called Ellie!"

"I couldn't ask you to come back unless we had a real plan. The real plan involved her changing her life. So I called her." He smiled briefly. "Plus, I wanted to ask for your hand."

She laughed. "Did you freak her out?"

"At first she was a bit shell-shocked, but when we got to talking about her future, she could see it."

She studied his face. "I almost can't believe this."

"Believe it. We've got some hurdles, and your daughter has some work to do. But we're going to make it."

She rose to her tiptoes and kissed him. "Yes. We are. Thank you."

He pulled her to him for a proper kiss, then he hugged her tightly and whispered in her ear, "Guess who's going to be Ellie's right-hand person?"

She pulled back so she could see his face.

"Sabrina."

She laughed. "What?"

"I've been saying she needed time and experience, and she wasn't getting it just traveling to charity events with me. I think she needs to see a nonprofit working from the inside out. We'll give her the summer off, and while she's at university for the next four years, her part-time job will be working for Ellie."

"Wow. This sort of works on a lot of levels, doesn't it?"

"Took me awhile to figure this one out, but I got it." He kissed her. "And I got the girl too."

She laughed.

He took a relieved breath. "Let's go home. I have an entire country I need to introduce you to."

EPILOGUE:
THEIR ROYAL WEDDING

THEY MARRIED TWO years later in Pocetak's huge, ornate cathedral. Serving as bridesmaids, Olivia, Sabrina and Ellie walked down the aisle.

In the two years of starting her nonprofit and easing herself into the public eye, the story of Ellie's assault had come and gone in the press. But the story of her nonprofit spread like wildfire. Especially that she was a strong, competent leader.

Ellie had her life back.

She easily walked down the aisle behind her two stepsisters in her beautiful peach dress. Not caring if anyone took her picture, smiling like the happy woman she had become.

Holding onto Josh's arm in the vestibule of the huge cathedral, Jessica took a quiet breath.

Josh put his hand over hers. "Nervous?"

"I shouldn't be. A lot of time and soul-searching went into this decision."

Josh snorted. "I knew from the first time I saw

you two together that you were meant for each other. That soul-searching was just a formality."

She laughed. "Maybe. Your dad *is* irresistible."

"And the funny thing is he never knew it. He was so wrapped up in his work that I don't think any woman ever caught his attention beyond a physical attraction."

"He's dedicated to your people, your country. I liked that about him immediately. That, Josh, is the kind of thing you look for when choosing a mate. Sexual attraction is good, but virtue is better."

Josh bent down and kissed her cheek. "You're such a mom. Luckily, I have years before I have to be that serious."

Trumpets sounded the first notes of the "Wedding March." Jessica looked down the aisle toward the altar where Mateo stood, looking wonderful in his military uniform, flanked by Arthur and Pete.

Life at the palace was different now that Mateo held a yearly ball thanking the employees and venturing out into the other offices to say hello and into the kitchen to compliment the chef.

Even though it felt like they were miles away from each other, she smiled at Mateo and he smiled back.

She and Josh started down the aisle. The closer she got the more her nervousness subsided. Who would have even thought that she'd be marrying a king or that that king would have been able to talk her and Ellie into coming out in public, starting a nonprofit and becoming heroes rather than victims.

They reached the altar. Josh kissed her cheek and handed her off to Mateo. She didn't have a veil. She hadn't worn a traditional wedding dress. She'd worn what she'd wanted: a big ball gown with a skirt that would flare out when they danced.

They said their vows, kissed to seal the deal and started down the aisle again, followed by their four kids. One who would be a queen. One who would run parliament. One who now was a victim's advocate. And one who was Ellie's assistant but who at twenty, still hadn't figured out her life.

But Jessica knew Sabrina would come up with something, a cause to champion or a business venture to run, and when she did she'd set the world on fire. She had too much of her dad in her not to.

For two people who'd had questionable first marriages, they had finally formed a real family where Ellie now had a dad and Mateo's kids now had a mom.

And everything really was right in their world.

* * * * *

Harlequin® Reader Service

Enjoyed your book?

Try the perfect subscription for Romance readers and get more great books like this delivered right to your door.

See why over 10+ million readers have tried Harlequin Reader Service.

Start with a Free Welcome Collection with free books and a gift—valued over $20.

Choose any series in print or ebook. See website for details and order today:

TryReaderService.com/subscriptions